GOING DOWN . . . HARD AND FAST!

"So much for canvassing the family," Fitzgibbon said as they headed for the elevator.

"It's harder than I expected," Frank said. "An angry sister and a brother who's very smooth."

"An angry sister who found the body," Fitzgibbon added. The doors to the private elevator opened, and they stepped inside.

"Let's not forget the main point, whether it got into the trial or not," Joe said. "The murder weapon turned up in Buff's possession."

He stabbed a finger at the button marked Lobby.

The doors closed, and Joe heard a grinding noise coming from above.

The elevator wasn't descending. It was *dropping*—plummeting out of control!

Nancy Drew & Hardy Boys SuperMysteries

DOUBLE CROSSING
A CRIME FOR CHRISTMAS
SHOCK WAVES
DANGEROUS GAMES
THE LAST RESORT
THE PARIS CONNECTION
BURIED IN TIME
MYSTERY TRAIN
BEST OF ENEMIES
HIGH SURVIVAL
NEW YEAR'S EVIL
TOUR OF DANGER
SPIES AND LIES
TROPIC OF FEAR
COURTING DISASTER
HITS AND MISSES
EVIL IN AMSTERDAM
DESPERATE MEASURES
PASSPORT TO DANGER
HOLLYWOOD HORROR
COPPER CANYON CONSPIRACY
DANGER DOWN UNDER
DEAD ON ARRIVAL
TARGET FOR TERROR
SECRETS OF THE NILE
A QUESTION OF GUILT

Available from ARCHWAY Paperbacks

A QUESTION OF GUILT

Carolyn Keene

AN ARCHWAY PAPERBACK
Published by POCKET BOOKS
New York London Toronto Sydney Tokyo Singapore

AN ARCHWAY PAPERBACK *Original*

An Archway Paperback published by
POCKET BOOKS, a division of Simon & Schuster Inc.
1230 Avenue of the Americas, New York, NY 10020

Produced by Mega-Books, Inc.

ISBN: 0-671-50293-X

First Archway Paperback printing March 1996

10 9 8 7 6 5 4 3 2 1

Cover art by Brian Kotzky

Printed in the U.S.A.

IL 6+

The Vidocq Society is an actual organization of law-enforcement professionals and forensic experts who donate their time and talents to uncover the solutions to unsolved crimes. This book is dedicated to all the members of the society, with special thanks to William Fleisher, Dr. Haresh Mirchandani, and Dr. Robert Goldberg, who so generously shared their expertise with the author. To quote the society's motto, *Veritas veritatum*—"Truth begets truth."

A QUESTION OF GUILT

Chapter One

"YOU SAID this bank robber had lots of guts but no brains." Joe Hardy gave a puzzled smile to the man across the table. "How'd you know that?"

Will Resnick, the Hardys' host for lunch, chuckled. "He was brave enough to try robbing a big bank at its busiest time. Hundreds of people were in there, cashing their paychecks. I guess he figured there'd be lots of money on hand."

A wicked grin crossed Resnick's craggy face. "And there certainly was. It was payday for the biggest tenant in that building—the New York office of the FBI."

Joe's father, Fenton Hardy, began to laugh. "Oh, yes! I heard about that would-be robber while I was still on the force in New York."

Joe's brother, Frank, nodded. "I remember reading about it. There were something like a hundred seventy-five agents waiting for the tellers."

"I was one of them." Resnick laughed again. "This pipsqueak pulls his gun, then we all pulled ours. I thought the poor guy was going to faint!"

"The guy sure didn't do his research," Joe said, laughing.

Joe enjoyed police war stories, and this was certainly the place for them. He, Frank, and their father had been invited as guests at a luncheon for members of the Vidocq Society, an organization of law-enforcement professionals and forensic experts. Joe found himself fascinated by the hundred or so people in the large private dining room that overlooked downtown Philadelphia. There were men and women, different races, and all ages represented.

They all seemed to have one thing in common, though, besides eating chicken parmesan with tomato sauce. Most of the people reminded him of his father. There was something about their eyes—a keen watchfulness combined with a sense that they'd seen it all.

Fenton Hardy had gotten that sharp expression from years in the New York City Police Department and his later career as a successful private investigator. He had the face of a veteran law enforcer.

Joe knew that he shouldn't be surprised that

the members of this club all had the same look. Dozens of police forces were represented here, not to mention the FBI and Special Agents of the Customs Department.

Will Resnick had proudly claimed that his group had experts in every kind of investigation, from accountants who traced dirty money, to psychologists who could track serial killers. The Vidocq Society could tackle any mystery.

"Dad says you're one of the founders of the Vidocq Society," Frank said.

"One of several people," Resnick quickly replied. "We all had different areas of expertise when it came to investigating. By putting our talents together, we hoped to find the answers to unsolved crimes."

"Why call it the Vidocq Society?" Joe asked as he cut a piece of chicken.

"Eugene Vidocq was a Frenchman who lived in the days of Napoleon," Resnick replied. "He pioneered the use of investigative methods to capture criminals, earning himself the title of the world's first detective."

Resnick glanced around the room. "Our members donate their time and talents to hunt down murderers and other criminals who might otherwise have gotten away. Sometimes, we also manage to clear innocent people who have been convicted unfairly." The older man smiled. "We tried to sum it up with our motto, *Veritas veritatum*—'Truth begets truth.'"

"They call you commissioner of the organization. The only commissioner I ever met ran the police in New York." Joe was joking, but he had to admit he was impressed by the Vidocq Society members he had met and their years of experience. Now Joe understood why his father was interested in joining the group, and why they'd come to Philadelphia for today's luncheon meeting. He relished listening to the stories Resnick and the other members told about cases they'd worked on. Joe just wished that he and Frank didn't have to go to Philadelphia to enjoy it.

The last time they'd visited that city, he and Frank were helping their father on a case. Fenton Hardy had been hired by the Bellamys, prominent Philadelphians, to investigate a murder in their family. But it had been Joe and Frank who'd unmasked the killer, prompted by police suspicions about one member of the Bellamy family.

Joe had heard of the young man before the case. Buford "Buff" Bellamy had appeared on the covers of several sports magazines. He was considered an up-and-coming star in American powerboat racing. But that was before the Hardys searched his car and found the murder weapon. Buff Bellamy had then become a famous fugitive, caught trying to escape by boat. And after his arrest, Buff became a celebrity defendant.

The Hardys had gone home, thinking they'd brought the investigation to a successful conclusion. Instead, Buff Bellamy had gotten off, and the newspapers had had a field day with the bungling "Hardy Boys."

Frank Hardy glanced over at Joe and noted his distracted expression. "Thinking about the last time we came down this way?" He kept his voice low, his dark eyes intent.

Joe nodded, eating the last bite of his chicken before replying. "That's why I'm leaving the war stories to everybody else," he said quietly. "I don't want to talk about that case. It's not enough that everybody thought we were idiots. We had to *know* the lawyer who made us look stupid." He scowled. "And of course it had to be the father of *your* special friend."

Frank's eyebrows rose. "*My* special friend? She's not your friend, too?"

"Right now, I'm not so sure," Joe said.

The waiter came to take their plates as Will Resnick rose and stepped over to a small lectern. "Good afternoon," he said into the microphone. "Thanks for attending. We have a number of interesting guests today, including Mr. Fenton Hardy, a private investigator from Bayport, and his sons, Frank and Joe."

With a touch of gray at his temples, Fenton Hardy looked every inch the professional as he rose and gave the group a little bow. Joe could feel his ears going red against his blond hair as he heard the buzz of whispered comments. Surely, the Philadelphians in the club hadn't forgotten a case only six months old. They had to be talking about the pair of kids who'd blown it.

Resnick cleared his throat, and the muttering died. "I have to make an announcement. As you know, we usually have a presentation for each meeting. Actually, we were going to discuss a murder case today, but we've run into a hitch. We asked a few questions of the police officer who was bringing the case to us. One of those initial questions suggested a new line of investigation, so we're leaving it in the hands of the local force."

He grinned at his fellow society members. "Although I'm sure we feel that's good news, it also means no case to talk about today. I was afraid I'd have to turn to our good friend Dr. Fell to fill the gap with one of his presentations on forensic medicine—"

"Another enjoyable lunch presentation of photos of dead bodies sliced up for autopsies!" a heavyset man said as he rose from one of the other tables.

That got a laugh from the group.

Resnick shot back. "But we're not going to let Dr. Fell do his stuff again until we have a lunch *without* tomato sauce." His mood suddenly became more serious. "At the last moment, we were approached with a new mystery. I talked it over with our case officer, Paul Shank. Although it may seem a bit . . . controversial to some members, I was quite impressed with our initial contact. The presenters should be here at any moment."

Joe noticed the headwaiter appear at the rear of the room. The man gave a discreet wave.

"Ah," Resnick said. "Here they come now."

The dining room door swung open, and in walked Carson Drew. Joe's jaw sagged in shock. Then he grit his teeth so hard, his head hurt. Carson Drew was the clever lawyer who'd gotten Buff Bellamy off.

Joe also recognized the person behind the attorney. "What's *she* doing here?" he whispered to his brother.

"I'm as surprised as you are," Frank replied.

Nancy Drew had as good a reputation for solving mysteries as the Hardys did. The boys had even worked together with her on some cases.

Joe knew his brother was very fond of Nancy. Joe liked her, too. They'd faced danger and put a lot of bad guys away. To have her father work for the other side, helping a murderer evade punishment—well, it felt like a betrayal to Joe.

But there was a bigger shock in store than just seeing the Drews.

Nancy turned back to the door and beckoned.

A tall, well-built, and very handsome blond guy appeared in the opening.

Joe wasn't the only one to gasp. His brother, his father, and several Philadelphia police officers were doing the same.

The newcomer was Buff Bellamy—the killer who'd gotten away with his crime!

BVM.231Y

Title:	A Question of Guilt (Nancy Drew & Hardy Boys Super Mysteries #26)
Cond:	Good
User:	jenb_list
Station:	DESKTOP-0NBMLBR
Date:	2025-01-25 14:25:49 (UTC)
Account:	Blue Vase Books
Orig Loc:	Aisle 30-Bay 8-Shelf 6
mSKU:	BVM.231Y
vSKU:	BVV.067150293X.G
Seq#:	714
unit_id:	25910757
width:	0.75 in
rank:	3,077,839
Cond Note:	Mass market paperback in GOOD condition with normal wear from use. Cover art my differ from that shown in photo.

BVV.067150293X.G

delist unit# 25910757

XXXXX

Chapter Two

"I DON'T BELIEVE THIS!" Frank Hardy muttered, staring at Nancy as she followed her father across the room to the podium. She passed near the table where the Hardys were sitting. As Buff Bellamy came closer, Joe got over his astonishment. His expression showed pure fury.

Reaching out, Frank clamped a hand on Joe's arm, and just in time. Joe was already starting to rise. Frank was able to restrain his brother until Buff had gone by.

"You've got to hand it to Bellamy," Joe growled. "He's got even more guts than Resnick's bank robber."

Frank nodded toward Carson Drew. "His lawyer has a lot more brains, though. Let's listen to what he has to say." He found himself staring at

Nancy and Buff as they stood together. Tall, blond, and good-looking, they seemed to make a perfect couple.

Will Resnick introduced the Drews and Buff. Then Carson Drew stepped up to the microphone. "I'd like to thank Mr. Resnick for his courtesy in inviting us today—and for his courage. I know that neither Mr. Bellamy nor I can be very popular with a lot of people in this room."

Frank glanced around. By his quick count, there were far more hostile eyes on the lawyer than friendly—or even neutral—ones.

Carson Drew wasn't a man to be scared off, though. "You may wonder why I'm here, since I got the charge against Mr. Bellamy dismissed without prejudice. But I'm not pressing my luck. Since the trial I've spoken long and hard with Buff, and so has my daughter, Nancy. We're both convinced that he's innocent. And we're asking for the help of the Vidocq Society to prove that fact."

The room went from dead silence to a dull roar of whispers, arguments, and protests. Frank heard Joe Hardy's heartfelt cry of "Oh, come on!"

Carson Drew rode the wave of noise, then gestured for silence. "As you know, the chief district attorney for Philadelphia is a member of Vidocq. She was the one who first suggested that I approach the society. Of course, the D.A. could always bring the charges against my client again if new evidence turns up. I turn to you because I believe any new evidence will clear Buff."

He scanned the assembly of law officers. Frank saw Mr. Drew's eyes flick in his direction and widen in surprise. Then he continued speaking. "I'm not blaming anyone or charging an official setup. But I do think that the police felt they'd been handed an open-and-shut case, so they didn't investigate all the possibilities."

Furious, Joe Hardy stirred in his seat. But Frank again held his brother back.

"Let's briefly go over what's known about the crime. Six months ago Laurel Kenway was stabbed to death in the Philadelphia mansion of her legal guardian, Stafford Bellamy. The president of Bellamy Holdings, Stafford was a major player in Philadelphia's real estate market. He died in an auto accident barely a month before the murder. It was his niece, Guinevere Bellamy, who brought in Fenton Hardy, whom I see is with us today."

Frank saw his father nod in silence.

"Fenton's sons, Frank and Joe, also became involved. The young men are themselves considered to be very good investigators."

In spite of the compliment, Joe glared at Nancy's father.

"At that point, there were certain rumors floating around the police department. Several officers suspected that something 'wasn't right' with the statement Buff Bellamy had provided about the murder. But aside from this gut feeling during questioning, there was nothing to go on. They certainly had no evidence strong enough to get a warrant and search for anything incriminating. The Hardys, however, heard these rumors, searched Buff's car, and discovered a bloody knife."

Joe gave a brief, savage nod. Frank, however, stared thoughtfully around. He realized that the whole room had gone silent. All the diners were concentrating on what Carson Drew had to say.

"Buff assures me he has no idea how the knife got into his car. But when the Hardys confronted him with it, he lost his head and ran. Buff was arrested, and the knife was shown to be the murder weapon. The prosecutor brought Buff to trial."

One of the members raised a hand. "Pardon me, Mr. Drew, could you explain your defense?"

Carson nodded. "It relied on an interesting point of law. If Frank and Joe Hardy had been police, their warrantless search would have been illegal. Then the knife couldn't have been used as evidence in the trial. The D.A. took the case to trial because the Hardys made the search as private citizens. But they did so after getting information—suspicions—from the police. That means they were acting as unofficial agents—cat's-paws—of the police. And the Supreme Court has ruled that such searches are not lawful."

"Legal mumbo jumbo," Joe muttered bitterly. Though his voice was low, the words seemed to echo in the room. Frank shot Nancy an embarrassed glance, but Carson quickly picked up on the words.

"Not mumbo jumbo," he said, "a constitutional protection. If a government starts dismantling the protections against unfair search and seizure, no citizen is safe. Police must *prove* there's a need to invade someone's home, office—or car."

Carson returned to the story. "Although some people may think very little of my argument, the judge agreed with me. He ruled that the knife and Buff's flight should be excluded from the trial. I know the local law is still trying to build a case to prove my client guilty. But I wouldn't waste your time asking for help unless I was sure of one thing. Your investigation *will* prove that Buff is innocent."

Carson Drew stepped back, and Will Resnick went to the podium. "I know we usually have a question-and-answer session, but I think we should mull over what we've just heard."

As the head of the society spoke, Nancy stepped over to take Resnick's seat. She leaned across the table, aiming an almost pleading look at the Hardys. "No one told us you guys would be here. I just want—"

"What? To gloat?" Joe burst out.

Frank realized his brother was angrier than he'd ever seen him. Again, Frank clamped a hand on Joe's arm. "Great to see you, Nancy," he said. "I've been thinking while I listened to your dad. And while I don't think the cops used us—"

"We acted on our own," Joe insisted.

"I don't think it would hurt to look at other angles," Frank continued.

Joe stared at him as if he'd just grown an extra head. But before Joe could say anything, another person went up to the microphone and began speaking.

"I—ah—I guess I should thank Mr. Drew for speaking so well for me." Buff Bellamy cleared his throat. "And Mr. Resnick for letting us come here in the first place. But there's something *I've* got to say." He looked around the room. "I know most of you think I'm a useless playboy—and a murderer. I'm not. But how can I convince you? I've thought a lot since I got hauled into jail. So I decided. Mr. Drew said you have all sorts of experts in this society. Is there somebody who knows about lie detectors?"

Nancy sucked in a long, unhappy breath. "He's doing this on his own," she said. "Neither my dad nor I suggested this."

Frank was surprised—but also impressed. Joe, however, looked like a wolf who'd just had a bloody steak thrown in front of him.

A tall, broad-shouldered man stood. "I have my equipment here."

Will Resnick turned to him. "Would you be free to do the test after the meeting today?"

"Sure," the man said. "No problem."

Resnick turned to Buff. "Why don't you two get together and work out the details?"

After making some concluding remarks, Resnick returned to the table. He looked down and smiled. "Well, Ms. Drew, I see you've stolen my seat."

"Mr. Resnick," Frank said, "will this case be the same as the ones you discussed during lunch?"

Resnick nodded. "We'll form an investigating team—"

"You said people didn't have to be members to help out," Frank said. "I'm on spring break, and I'd like to lend a hand. What about you, Joe?" He turned to his brother.

Joe Hardy thought for a moment. Then his mouth curved up in a slow smile. "Count me in."

"Me, too," Nancy said firmly.

As soon as the luncheon meeting broke up, Frank, Joe, Nancy, Will Resnick, and the lie detector examiner, who was introduced as Ross McGarry, went to Buff's room at the Fairview Hotel. The Hardys, Nancy, and Will Resnick stood by as McGarry connected several pieces of equipment to Buff's body. A pair of rubber tubes went around his chest and upper stomach. Next McGarry slipped what looked like a blood-pressure cuff onto Buff's arm. Then came odd, glovelike coverings for the index and ring fingers of one hand.

Each of these hookups was attached by wire to a briefcase-size device that McGarry had set up on a table. There were some switches and controls, but what caught Joe's attention was the roll of paper and the four thin metal arms with pens at the end.

"So this box is the machine, huh?" Joe asked, bending over to peer at the apparatus.

McGarry looked as if someone had just spit on his baby. "That's the instrument, or the polygraph," he corrected Joe frostily.

Resnick spoke up. "I'm afraid 'box' and 'machine' are police slang for polygraphs. Professionals like Mr. McGarry prefer to use the term 'instrument'—just as he's an examiner, not an operator."

McGarry checked the mechanism. The paper began to roll, and the pens started jiggling.

"Each pen records a physical reaction," Resnick explained. "The straps check Buff's breathing at the chest and at the diaphragm. The cuff measures his heart rate and blood pressure."

"And the things on his fingers?" Joe asked.

"That's to pick up electrodermal responses—

which change with perspiration," Resnick said. "Believe it or not, the palm sides of your fingers have the most sweat glands per square inch of anywhere on your body."

"So you're saying that's a sweat-meter?" Joe shook his head.

"I used to think that polygraph was some fancy word for lie-finder," Frank said to Nancy. "But it turns out to be Greek for 'lots of writing.'"

"Well, it's sure doing that," she said, watching the pens wiggle along the paper as McGarry asked Buff a series of yes-or-no questions. Frank knew that these were designed to set up a baseline, a yardstick to let McGarry measure Buff's later responses.

Nancy watched with a slightly nervous expression. "It's not foolproof," she said to Frank. "The machine—instrument—measures *emotional* response, not the truth."

"I've heard stories about people managing to beat the test by leaning against a tack hidden in their shoes," Frank admitted.

"Then let's get his shoes off." Joe definitely wasn't joking.

But Buff had already kicked off his footwear. "Hope you don't mind me making myself comfortable," he said.

"Fine with me." McGarry glanced at his audience. "Can you give us some room?"

Resnick led the teens to the far side of the hotel room. They could still hear, but they wouldn't be heard if they kept their voices down.

"Polygraph examiners usually have two techniques to choose from," Resnick said. "One looks for guilty knowledge—in this case, something only the killer would know. The problem is, a lot of that information came out as the trial came up."

"What's the other method?" Frank asked.

"Control and relevant questions," Resnick replied. "You might call it the general versus the particular. Say you wanted to find out if someone stole money. Your control question would be, 'Have you ever stolen anything in your life?' "

He smiled. "The relevant question might be, 'Did you make the money disappear from the cash register on Thursday?' With those squiggly lines, a good examiner can get the subject's body to betray himself—or herself."

McGarry spent perhaps half an hour working with Buff, acting almost as if he were chatting with the suspect. From time to time, he flicked a marker on the rolling sheet of paper. Finally, McGarry rose from his seat and strolled over to the observers.

"I came at the murder from several different directions," McGarry reported. "There was no indication that he did it."

At Frank's shoulder, Nancy gave a sigh of relief as the examiner went on. "The only questionable response was to a control question—'Did you quarrel with Laurel Kenway in the year before she died?' "

Frank caught a glimpse of abrupt, violent movement from the corner of his eye. Joe was shaking his head. "He's bluffing his way out of this somehow."

If McGarry had been annoyed before, he was angry now. "You want to see how it feels?" he demanded. "I can test *you* and see how you fake it."

"All right," Joe snapped, nose to nose with the polygraph man.

Frank coughed, trying to hide a chuckle. How else would his kid brother respond to a challenge?

In moments Buff was out of the lie-detection gear and Joe was in it. Buff went down to the hotel restaurant, but Frank and Nancy stayed, feeding McGarry information for the baseline questions. Then the polygraph examiner turned to them. "Anything in particular you want to know about this character?"

Frank raised an eyebrow and smiled gleefully, "Control question, then the relevant one, right?"

McGarry nodded.

"Ooo-kay," Frank said, thinking for a second. "Have you ever played a practical joke?"

Joe stared at him. "Sure."

"Were you the one who sewed up Chet Morton's sweatpants in gym class?"

"Hey, come on!" Joe protested.

"Just yes or no answers," McGarry interjected.

Joe glared. "No."

"Hmmm," McGarry said, watching the paper roll. "His breathing stopped for a second, and his heart rate increased. Reasonable indications that he's not telling the truth."

"You didn't do this with Bellamy," Joe complained.

"That's because Buff was telling the truth," Nancy said. "And he didn't call this instrument a box." She turned to Frank. "My turn?"

"Be my guest," Frank said.

There was an impish twinkle in Nancy's blue eyes. "So, Joe," she said sweetly, "ever cheated on a girlfriend?"

"What kind of question—" Joe furiously began, but was cut off by the examiner.

"Yes or no."

"No!" The answer came out as a shout.

McGarry's eyebrows rose. "It's not often you see *all* the pens register like that."

"Is that the one for sweating?" Nancy asked, pointing. "Oh, look! It's still going up." She glanced at Joe. "Your girlfriend Vanessa might be interested in the next question."

"Give me a break . . . *please?"*

Frank was amazed to hear his brother almost begging.

"Okay," Nancy said unexpectedly. "If you'll

promise to help out with the Vidocq investigation—one hundred percent."

"You got it," Joe said.

"Then we're all agreed," Frank said with relief. "Everything's cool."

His relief faded, however, when he saw the polygraph needles swinging madly.

"Sure, I'll help you," Joe said. "Because I'm going to prove Buff Bellamy is guilty as sin!"

Chapter Three

NANCY TURNED a little anxiously to Will Resnick, who'd been watching the by-play. "I hope you don't think we're just fooling around." After struggling to get the Vidocq Society's help, Nancy didn't want to be left out of the investigation.

The commissioner of the Vidocq Society didn't seem upset, though. In fact, he laughed. "Solving crimes is a grim business," Resnick said. "And pretty intense," he added, glancing at Joe. "I for one don't mind enjoying a lighter moment."

As McGarry began packing up his equipment, Resnick turned to the three teens. "But now it's time to get serious again. Why don't we join our case officer, Paul Shank, and see who else has volunteered their services?"

They left the hotel and headed for the offices of the Customs Service on Chestnut and Second Streets. Nancy knew that Resnick and Shank were both Customs Special Agents. They were investigators who had distinguished themselves in other law-enforcement agencies and now tackled drug cases.

They walked down a bustling, crowded, and, Nancy thought, *narrow* street. It was barely three cars wide. She had to remind herself that while Walnut Street was an important Philadelphia thoroughfare, this part of the city dated back to the 1700s. The city was a lot smaller then.

They arrived at the U.S. Customhouse and went upstairs. Paul Shank looked up from his desk. "A lot of people came up to me after the meeting. Some FBI guys and several guys from Jersey volunteered. But most of our Philadelphia police members felt they couldn't join in."

"Well, we have a couple of people who were involved in the original investigation." Resnick gestured toward the Hardys.

"Maybe this time we'll get to the bottom of this case," Joe said.

"You make it sound as though we're going to haul everyone in for interrogation." Shank shook his head.

Joe looked a little surprised. "Well, you are a bunch of high-powered law-enforcement types."

"But remember, Vidocq has no official standing," Shank said. "Our people work as private citizens. We've contacted Buff's brother and sister. Ed Fitzgibbon is seeing Gwen Bellamy at the family mansion tomorrow, then Cris Bellamy at his office. We thought that you boys could join him. And, Nancy, one of our member medical examiners will be going over the coroner's report. We thought you could meet with him. I'll call you tonight with more details."

"Sounds good," Nancy said.

Resnick gave the Hardys and Nancy a crooked smile. "I just hope we can avoid the press. We'll get a lot more work done without a media circus."

"Well, we have some work to do ourselves," Frank said. "Joe and I had better start scaring up a hotel room if we're going to stick around."

"And it's certainly *not* going to be the Fairview," Joe muttered, referring to the hotel where Nancy and Buff had their rooms.

The next morning Nancy stood in Buff's room, growing more and more furious as she read the newspaper Buff had just given her. The headline told it all, in screaming letters—"Kenway Murder Investigation Reopened."

Nancy wasn't thinking about the problems caused by the publicity for the Vidocq investigators. She was concerned about Buff, who was obviously distressed.

"I thought this would all die down." Buff couldn't hide the bitterness in his voice. "Looks like I was wrong. It's starting all over again."

Nancy looked down at the paper. Buff's photo was just under the headline. Nancy recognized it as the photo that had been taken right after Buff's arrest. He looked tired, disheveled, and sullen.

"I called down to the main desk," he continued. "They said there's a mob of photographers and press people gathering outside."

"Buff—" Nancy began, but the young man cut her off, his voice quiet but stony.

"My whole life has been on hold for the last six months," Buff said. "I gave up racing and looked for a real job. But who's going to hire a murderer, even if the court didn't nail me? The charges were 'dismissed without prejudice.'" He quoted the legal jargon with the skill of one who'd learned it the hard way. "That means I'm off the hook for the time being—but they can still prosecute me again."

"I thought your brother offered you a job," Nancy said.

"Yeah—head paper-folder at Bellamy Holdings." Scorn crept into Buff's voice. "Cris can pull strings at the office now. When my uncle's will goes through, he'll end up running the company. He offered me executive pay for a job a temp worker could do. I turned it down."

Buff sighed. "The only good thing was that the press was finally off my back. The story had gone stale. But it seems I'm news again now—and you can bet they'll want fresh pictures." He glanced at Nancy. "I'll have to get out of here."

She nodded. "You're right," she said. "I have an idea, but I'll need an hour or so to work it out. In the meantime, don't leave the room." Nancy handed Buff the paper, then turned toward the door. "And while I'm gone," she added, "pack up your things."

Nancy was walking out the door as Buff asked, "You've really got a plan?"

Nancy smiled. "I *hope* I've got one."

When Nancy returned an hour later, Buff was packed. Nancy gestured to the two suitcases on the bed. "That's all you've got?"

"I travel light. Most of my stuff is at Uncle Stafford's place on Rittenhouse Square," Buff said. "I couldn't sleep in the mansion anymore. Not after Laurel—" His voice broke. "Not after Laurel died there."

"We'll put your bags in my room," Nancy said. "If we're going to ditch those people outside, we can't be carrying luggage."

Nancy smoothed down the black skirt she was wearing. "You're wearing black pants. That's good."

"It is?" But Buff got no answer as he shrugged into a leather jacket, then carried his bags to Nancy's room down the hall. She selected a raincoat from her closet, donned it, then led the way to the elevator.

A loud chime rang through the elevator car as the doors opened on the main lobby. Buff gave Nancy a doubtful look. "I thought we'd be heading for the basement—the parking garage."

"And you can bet most of the media vultures expect you to drive out, too," Nancy replied. "Where do you think they're going to be?"

As they stepped out into the lobby, Buff directed nervous glances around. "This is a pretty public place," he muttered. "The management may be able to keep the guys with cameras out. But they've got to let people in. Some of the smarter paparazzi have staffs. You can be sure they've got spies in here."

Nancy knew about paparazzi, the professional photographers who pestered celebrities and newsmakers. Most of their work wound up on the covers of the sleazier supermarket tabloids. A shot of Buff would mean big bucks for these pros. Could Nancy beat them? She was about to find out.

Pausing for a second, Nancy scanned the lobby, looking for anyone who didn't seem to belong. The Fairview was an upscale hotel, with large mirrors, marble columns, and large, lush potted plants. Most of the people who stayed there were conservative and well-dressed. When Nancy spotted a man in cheap, flashy clothes talking to one of the bellmen, she was instantly on the alert.

She turned away but was able to keep an eye on the two—or rather, their reflection in one of the big wall mirrors. A couple of bills passed from the man into the hand of the hotel employee. He pointed to Buff, and the bribed bellman nodded. The flashily dressed man moved to cover the front entrance of the hotel. The bellman casually started walking toward Nancy and Buff.

Nancy hid a smile. "Okay, Buff. Follow my lead. And whatever I tell you to do, just do it, okay? No questions."

Buff blinked in surprise as Nancy hooked an arm around his elbow. "You're the boss," he said as she steered.

Nancy started for the rear of the lobby, away from the entrance. The bellman trailed after. They headed for the hotel's dining room, which was nearly empty. A few people sat over cups of coffee, but the restaurant's breakfast time had just ended, and it was hours before lunch.

Although the place was officially closed, the manager waved them in. Nancy risked a quick look over her shoulder. Yes, their shadow was staring after them as they headed straight for the kitchen. Like every hotel employee, he had to know that there was a service exit, if only for the removal of kitchen garbage.

Nancy glanced back again through the glass

window in the kitchen's swinging door. The bellman was rushing to make his report.

Quickly, Nancy took off her raincoat. "Get out of your jacket," she commanded.

Buff stared. "What?"

"No questions, remember?" Nancy yanked the leather coat off his shoulders. Even as she moved, a waiter and waitress walked up to her. They were both blond and, at a quick glance, resembled Nancy and Buff.

Nancy tossed her coat to the girl and finally got Buff out of his jacket. "Got anything important in the pockets?" she asked.

"Uh—no." Buff seemed almost in a daze at the quick turn of events.

"The coats will come back to my room when they're finished," Nancy promised with a grin. She tossed Buff a waiter's jacket and slipped into one of the waitress's vests. The hotel staffers had already donned the coats. Nancy turned up the collars and handed each of them a twenty-dollar bill. "You know what to do?"

The waitress nodded. "Head out the kitchen exit, don't let them see our faces, and run for the corner."

"Perfect." Nancy grinned. As the paparazzi were about to find out, they weren't the only ones who knew a little bribery could work wonders.

Turning, Nancy pushed Buff over to a room-service cart. "Bend over a bit, and keep your head down," she said.

They wheeled the cart out into the lobby and toward the service elevator. Although Nancy kept her head down, she looked to the left, then to the right. No one seemed to be paying attention to them. They'd vanished into the faceless mass of service staff. Nancy suddenly swung the cart down the empty corridor near the service elevator.

"We can ditch the cart," she whispered. "Come on!"

At the end of the corridor was a fire door. A large sign warned of all the alarms they'd set off if they pushed on the panic bar. Nancy took a deep breath. The manager had promised the alarms would be off for five minutes. Otherwise, they might as well try to exit with a brass band.

She pushed—and the door opened silently. Nancy and Buff stepped outside into an alleyway. Almost a block away, photographers were yelling.

"Buff! Hold on a minute! Give us a picture!" one of the photographers shouted.

"Look this way, Buff!" screamed another.

"Who's the girl?" a third media hound wanted to know.

Huddling in their borrowed coats, Nancy's decoys dashed around the corner. The paparazzi roared off in pursuit.

Nancy and Buff turned their backs and headed down the block. There, just at the mouth of the alley, was the rental limousine Nancy had arranged to have waiting.

"We did it!" Nancy said. "We fooled them all!"

Buff sped up, eager to get into the limo and away. They were almost there when the small compact car parked in front of the limo seemed to erupt. The door flew open, and out stepped a plump man dressed in a safari suit that was a little too tight for him. The outfit had no place in the Philadelphia streets, suggesting the man was from out of town, and the big, heavy news camera he snatched from the car seat showed why he was there. The man was a paparazzo. He'd spotted the limo and staked it out.

Nancy whipped around, dragging Buff with her.

"Well," she said through gritted teeth, "we fooled *most* of them."

Chapter Four

THE PHOTOGRAPHER ADVANCED almost casually, a big grin on his pockmarked face. "Come on, Buff," he called, raising his camera. "Y'ain't going nowhere without me gettin' the picture."

His words were cut off, however, by the roar of a car engine. A slightly dented, nondescript car made a screeching turn into the alley. The paparazzo jumped to one side, afraid of being hit by the careening vehicle.

By doing that, the photographer missed his one chance for a shot. The junker lurched to a stop, and the rear door swung open, revealing the grinning face of Frank Hardy. Joe was driving.

"Hey!" the photographer yelled as his targets piled into the car. Buff crouched on the floor, leaving the photographer without a subject.

Nancy bounced onto the backseat and slammed the door just as Joe Hardy hit the gas.

They quickly outdistanced the furious photographer. Frank watched out the back window. The paparazzo dashed for his car. But even as he moved, the limousine surged to life, blocking the mouth of the alley. Mr. Photographer wouldn't be able to turn and pursue them.

"Heads down, everybody!" Joe said sharply.

They reached the corner where the paparazzi had congregated. Joe knew the media vultures should still be chasing Nancy's decoys. But they might have already discovered the trick and be heading back.

Nancy joined Buff on the floor. Frank ducked, worrying. What if a photographer took Joe's blond hair for Buff's and started a new charge? When Nancy called for help, Frank had planned on driving. But that would have left Joe huddled in the backseat with a girl who'd annoyed him and a guy he hated.

So Frank had put Joe behind the wheel, wearing a newly purchased hat to hide his hair.

Up ahead, Joe executed a turn and glanced in his rearview mirror. "All clear," he reported.

The three passengers cautiously raised their heads to peek out the back windshield. They had left the hotel behind and were now zigzagging through the maze of narrow one-way streets that made up downtown Philadelphia.

"Nice car," Nancy commented, giving Frank a mock glare as she brushed dust off herself.

"It's the best wreck money could rent," Frank assured her, grinning. "After all, I didn't know how much damage we'd take from charging reporters. The car I got for you guys is much nicer."

"For us?" Buff couldn't quite seem to catch up with what was going on.

"A good getaway is like a magic trick," Nancy explained. "The most important part is misdirection—getting the audience, in this case those newspeople, to watch the wrong things."

"Like dressing those two hotel workers to look like us," Buff said.

"Right." Nancy nodded. "But I couldn't be sure everybody would go off on a wild-goose chase. So I hired a limo to distract anyone who didn't fall for my decoys."

"You didn't expect to use it?" Buff asked in disbelief.

"Not unless we were very, very lucky," Nancy admitted. "And we weren't."

"So we picked you up," Frank said. "That photographer we skunked saw you escape in a gray junker." He grinned. "Pretty soon, that's what all the news people will be looking for. So what you need is a different car."

"More misdirection," Nancy said.

Buff shook his head, staring at Nancy in disbelief. "You set all this up this morning?"

Nancy shrugged. "I was just lucky that there were some guys in town I could rely on." She smiled at the Hardys. "Thanks, Frank . . . Joe."

"Yeah," Buff agreed. "Thanks, guys."

"Don't sweat it," Frank said.

From the front seat, Joe's reaction sounded more like a strangled growl.

Frank saw Nancy straighten up, as if she'd just sat on a pin. "You know," she muttered to Frank, "that attitude of your brother's gets old—very fast."

"Um, yeah." Frank could feel his face getting red as he dug in his pocket. "Here are the keys to your car. We're almost there."

Joe pulled up at the side of the road with a jerk. Frank pointed out the window to a late-model rental car. "Where will you be headed?"

"I don't know," Buff admitted. "I've been living with friends down in Florida. But I want to stay in Philadelphia for the investigation."

"Your uncle has an estate in the suburbs, doesn't he?" Nancy said.

Buff nodded. "It's in the town of Orbeck—maybe half an hour's drive from here."

"That sounds like the place to go." Nancy paused at the expression on Buff's face. "You can guide me, can't you?"

"It's just that my sister is staying there," Buff said. "She won't be happy to see me."

Frank glanced up. "You don't have to worry about that. She's supposed to be in town today.

We're meeting one of the Vidocq investigators—"

"And we're supposed to be doing it *soon.*" Joe tapped significantly on his watch.

Nancy opened her door. "Let's get going." Her voice was flat.

As Nancy and Buff drove off, Frank joined his brother in the rental car's front seat. "You were awfully generous with the attitude," he said.

"I'm going along on the investigation," Joe replied. "I don't have to like the guy."

They drove to the customhouse, where Paul Shank introduced them to the investigator they'd be accompanying. "Frank and Joe Hardy, Ed Fitzgibbon."

Fitzgibbon was a tall, lanky man, whose skin seemed stretched tight over the bones of his face. "I knew your father," he said in a slightly raspy voice. "We were both on the force in New York. He left to go private. I moved to a smaller town—Conway, New Jersey."

"Ed runs the Criminal Investigation Bureau for the Conway police," Shank explained.

"It's not the biggest town, but we still get murders," Fitzgibbon said. He led the boys downstairs to an unmarked car that was almost as shabby as the Hardys' rented vehicle.

"They'll love seeing this wreck parked around Rittenhouse Square," Fitzgibbon joked.

Frank grinned. They were heading for one of the most elegant areas in the city. Rittenhouse

Square was a beautifully manicured park surrounded by high-rise apartment buildings and expensive hotels. But on the side streets around the park were mansions more than a century old. Some had been turned into offices and boutiques. Others were still the homes of Philadelphia's first families. The Bellamy place was a solid three-story brick mansion with seven-foot-tall white-trimmed windows. It was twice as wide as any other house on the block.

Fitzgibbon managed to find a parking space on the park. As they walked to the house, the investigator said to the Hardys, "I'd appreciate it if you guys would let me run the interrogation."

"Interrogation?" Joe pounced angrily on the word. "You make her sound like a suspect."

"I thought we were just looking for more information," Frank said a little more tactfully.

"We *are* looking for information—about a murder," Fitzgibbon replied. "That means asking questions. And like it or not, we have to investigate the family. A lot of murders get solved close to home."

"But Gwen Bellamy hired our dad," Joe protested. "That's why we were down here in the first place."

"So she knows you, which ought to help us get started," Fitzgibbon said. "She may not like some of the questions I'll ask. We're dealing with a case that's getting cold, so I'll have to shake things up." He gave the boys a tight smile. "Look at it this way. If I annoy these folks, it will be all my fault."

Frank and Joe exchanged glances. "Okay," Frank said. "You're the expert."

When they rang the doorbell of the mansion, Frank expected a butler to answer the door. Instead, they were met by a slim young man in casual but expensive clothes. He had a chiseled face, just a little too narrow to be considered handsome. He brushed back stylishly cut dark hair as he looked at them. "Yes?" he asked.

"We were told Miss Guinevere Bellamy would be here—" Fitzgibbon began, only to be interrupted.

"What is it, Lawrence? More reporters?" Guinevere Bellamy appeared behind the young man. Her light brown hair had grown longer in the months since Frank had seen her, but she had the same good looks as her younger brother, Buff.

Gwen obviously recognized Frank and Joe, too. Her blue eyes seemed to freeze over as she looked at them. "So," she said coldly, "the article in the paper was right. My brother the murderer managed to start a new investigation."

Her words threw off even the experienced Fitzgibbon. "We have a few questions—"

"I've changed my mind about the interview; I dealt with enough questions the last time around," Gwen Bellamy cut him off. "The answers didn't exactly please me, but I've had to live with them. My brother is guilty—and I'm not going to let him ruin my life again!"

With those words, Gwen slammed the door shut.

"Do we ring the bell again?" Joe asked.

"I don't see the use," Fitzgibbon admitted. He glanced at the Hardys. "I was saving you two in case we had to play good cop–bad cop. But I guess that wouldn't work with this young woman. To her mind, it seems all cops are bad."

"So what do we do now?" Frank asked.

"Let's find a phone and give Crispin Bellamy a call," Fitzgibbon said. "We'll see if we can move up our meeting."

They found a pay phone, and Fitzgibbon punched in a number. After a brief conversation, he turned to the boys. "We've been invited to join him for lunch," the detective announced.

"You don't look happy," Frank said.

Fitzgibbon shrugged. "I was hoping to get down to South Philly and have a cheesesteak," he admitted.

"A what?" Joe said.

"A cheesesteak," Fitzgibbon answered. "Thinly sliced beef grilled with cheese and onions, served on a hero roll."

"Sounds great." Joe licked his lips.

"But instead, we'll be stopping off at your hotel so you can change into dress shirts and ties."

Joe looked down at his chinos and blue work-shirt. "What's wrong with what we have on?"

"It won't do for the fancy-shmancy place we're going," Fitzgibbon assured them. "I've been to these dining clubs before."

The investigator explained as they drove to the boys' hotel, the Stratford, on Broad Street. "Back when I was a young fella, there were hardly any restaurants in Philadelphia. The society types all ate in these private clubs. Anyone else who wanted a meal ate at home or off a pushcart."

"Sounds pretty snobbish to me," Frank said.

"In New York, they ask what you're worth. In this town, it's who you know." Fitzgibbon shrugged. "Society people can act like a different tribe. And remember, the Bellamys are society people with a capital *S.*"

Frank began to see what the investigator meant after they'd changed and arrived at the Rooftop Club. The place was located in the penthouse of a large but ancient office building. To reach the club, they had to ride in a private elevator. When they arrived, the manager led them to a glass-walled room where all the tables were turned away from the downtown view.

"It's probably considered low-class to gawk at the view," Fitzgibbon muttered.

A young man rose from his table to greet them. Crispin Bellamy was only twenty-five, but his dark suit and quiet tie was the uniform of a veteran business executive. Frank had noticed the strong family resemblance among the Bellamys during the earlier case. Cris looked like a copy of his younger brother, except that his hair was sandy instead of bright blond and his body slimmer.

"Please sit down. Order anything you like—that's one of the perks of being a big shot." He grinned, making fun of himself. "Although for me, that seems to mean ten- and twelve-hour days. The firm is working on several big land deals. We've got to prove ourselves after losing Uncle Stafford."

Frank took care of the introductions. The boys and Fitzgibbon sat down and were immediately handed menus. They quickly ordered club sandwiches, french fries, and soft drinks.

"In a way, I'm glad you changed your schedule. I wouldn't have had much time at the office—not that I've got a lot of time now." Cris glanced at his watch.

"You can thank your sister," Joe said.

Cris Bellamy looked embarrassed. "She refused to see you at all? I was afraid of that." He turned to Fitzgibbon. "This whole thing has been a disaster for her. She had to put off her wedding when our uncle died in a car crash."

"Yes, we're looking into that crash," Joe said. "Do you know where the limo ended up?"

"Why—no," Cris replied, startled. "I'm afraid

we didn't pay much attention, what with the funeral. Then came the whole unpleasantness with Buff. Now, when she starts planning her wedding again, *this* begins," Cris said. "I'm happy to do anything to help Buff, but Gwen . . . blames him. She's even gone to court, tying up our uncle's will. Gwen wants Buff cut out of the inheritance."

"Your uncle left a pretty big estate?" As Fitzgibbon spoke, he directed stern looks toward the Hardys. Frank remembered that the investigator wanted to ask the questions. Their food arrived, and he decided to eat in silence.

Cris took a bite of his cheeseburger before answering. "There's the company, of course, the mansions here in town and in Orbeck, stocks and other assets. My interest is in the business. I've worked for Uncle Stafford since I graduated from college. Got a civil engineering degree." Cris grinned again. "It helps to know how buildings stay up if you're going to work in real estate."

Fitzgibbon nodded as he speared a french fry with his fork. "I suppose you know why we're here."

Crispin Bellamy immediately looked serious. "It's about Laurel," he said. "How sad to bring it all up again. I don't know what more I can tell you. When I made my statement to the police, they seemed pretty thorough."

"I'd still like to hear you tell about the night Laurel Kenway was murdered," Fitzgibbon said.

Frank was surprised at the man's tone. He seemed almost to be pushing Cris.

"There's really not much to tell," Bellamy said. "I was working late in the office when I got a call from Gwen. She'd just come home and found Laurel—the body."

"What were you working on?" Fitzgibbon asked.

"A building claim from a contractor," Cris answered promptly. "We had to change the plans on the project, and the contractor was complaining that it would cost him a lot of money. He even hired some hotshot consultant to back up his claims with charts and graphs. I was going over all this stuff because we had a meeting with our lawyers the next morning."

"Were you working with anyone?" Fitzgibbon pressed.

Cris frowned. "Well, no, not exactly. But I was in and out of Mr. Tacey's, briefing him on some of the fine points. That's Richard Tacey—he's head of operations at the firm. He had the final call, deciding how aggressive our lawyers would be."

"So, how often were you in his office?"

The young man hesitated, pushing his french fries around on his plate. "Four—maybe five times. I'm not sure after all these months." He took another bite of his cheeseburger.

"Do you think Tacey might remember?"

"I couldn't say—oh, no!" Cris rose from his

seat. "I left a note on Mr. Tacey's desk last night about a problem, and I need to check in with him. Excuse me a minute." He hurried off.

"What's with the third degree?" Joe asked Fitzgibbon. "You're coming down on him pretty hard. At least Cris is talking to us—unlike his snotty sister."

The detective frowned. "Yeah. But only about certain things, like how his sister is screwing things up. But he was evasive when we got around to the murder. He couldn't even say that Laurel Kenway had been killed."

"What do you mean?" Frank put down his turkey club sandwich and regarded the detective.

"I asked if he knew why we were here. He didn't say it was because of the murder, or the killing. He answered, 'Because of Laurel.'"

"That's a clue?" Joe said skeptically.

"Every answer is a clue," Fitzgibbon said. "Look at how Cris described Gwen's discovery. Most people would say, 'She found Laurel dead,' or 'She saw Laurel had been killed.'"

Joe slowly nodded. "But he said she came home and found Laurel's body."

"Not exactly," Frank said. "He said 'Laurel—the body,' avoiding the mention of murder."

"And he was very quick with his alibi until I began picking at it," Fitzgibbon went on.

Bellamy came rushing over, the manager trailing behind. "Gentlemen, I'm sorry. There's a bit of a crisis at the office. We're selling a shopping center down in Chester, and I got a call from the purchaser late yesterday saying he was concerned about the floor tiles." Cris made a face. "Today he's got a consultant's report saying *all* the floors are no good, and so he wants to knock six hundred thousand dollars off our price. I have to run." He took the bill from the manager and signed it. "Why don't you stay and finish up—have dessert and coffee if you like."

Fitzgibbon looked long and hard at the young man. "I hope we can continue our discussion."

"Of course—certainly," Cris promised, backing away. "Just let me get out from under this. You can catch me at the office." Then he was gone.

Fitzgibbon looked down at his plate. "Let me share something I've noticed over the years. People who don't want to give much away in an interrogation always try to limit how much time you spend questioning them."

"Cris certainly did that," Frank had to admit.

"Maybe it runs in the family," Joe said. "The Philly cops didn't like the way Buff answered their questions. And talk about limiting time—Gwen wouldn't let us speak to her at *all.*"

"There is that." Fitzgibbon shrugged.

"Maybe they're all holding something back," Frank suggested. "Family secrets?"

"Well, they couldn't all have done it together," Joe said. "That kind of stuff only happens in weirdo mystery movies."

They finished their meal and decided against dessert.

"So much for canvassing the family," Fitzgibbon said as they headed for the elevator.

"It's harder than I expected," Frank said. "An angry sister and a brother who's very smooth."

"An angry sister who found the body," Fitzgibbon added.

"But she hired our dad to investigate the murder," Joe protested.

"The perfect way to avoid suspicion," Fitzgibbon pointed out. The doors to the private elevator opened, and they stepped inside.

"Let's not forget the main point, whether it got into the trial or not," Joe said. "The murder weapon turned up in Buff's possession."

He stabbed a finger at the button marked Lobby.

The doors closed, and he heard a grinding noise coming from above.

The elevator wasn't descending. It was *dropping*—plummeting out of control!

Chapter Five

NANCY DREW CAREFULLY HEFTED the two thick manila envelopes in her hands.

"The heavier one is the medical examiner's file on Laurel Kenway," Will Resnick told her. "Some society members here in Philadelphia were able to get it. We're lucky the Montgomery County coroner could send over their file on Stafford Bellamy so quickly."

"I think our pal Dr. Fell called in some sort of favor." Paul Shank gave Nancy an appreciative nod. "I'm glad you thought of it when I called you yesterday."

Nancy shrugged. "When one person dies, you don't immediately think of foul play. But when a second person dies—a person with a strong connection to the first one—maybe it's time for a little suspicion."

"Gabriel Fell is tops in his field," Resnick said. "If there's anything out of place in either of those reports, he'll spot it."

"Then the sooner he gets them, the better." Nancy tucked the bulky folders under her arm. "Just call me Drew's Delivery Service. I shuttled Buff off to Orbeck this morning. Now I'll take these—where?"

A second later Nancy realized what the answer to her question would be. After all, where did medical examiners usually hang out? Morgues. Not exactly my favorite kind of place to hang out, Nancy reminded herself.

"Doc Fell is here in town," Will Resnick said. "He's using some space at a forensic—"

Here it comes, Nancy thought.

"Sculptor's," Resnick finished.

"Ah," Nancy said. She'd heard of forensic sculptors—artists who used their talents to reconstruct the appearance of unidentified murder victims, sometimes from a mere handful of physical clues.

"Phil Varenza. He's a member of the society with a studio on Society Hill, just south of the center city."

Nancy took down the address, then headed for her rental car. She soon found herself gliding down the streets of a quiet residential area. The sidewalks were brick, and so were most of the houses. Ancient trees cast shade on homes that had to be two hundred years old. But before she felt as though she'd gone through a time warp, Nancy passed a block of new townhouses, cleverly designed to fit in with their older neighbors.

Nancy found the address she was looking for, parked the car, and got out. She looked up at the house. It had to date back to the Revolutionary War, she thought. The house had been lovingly restored, and its mellow brick walls seemed to glow. The wooden window frames were painted a brilliant white, which contrasted with the green of the doors and shutters. Nancy used a brass door knocker, and a slim, bearded man answered. He smiled as Nancy introduced herself.

"You're looking for my partner in crime, Dr. Fell," the man said. "I'm Phil Varenza. Forgive me for not shaking hands—they're full of clay."

He led the way to the rear of the house, where a surprisingly modern art studio overlooked a small garden. On a waist-high metal counter stood a half-finished clay sculpture, a head with blurred features. Beside it was a human skull. Photos and drawings of the skull filled a corkboard along one wall.

A man sitting at a plain wooden table by the window rose as Nancy came into the room. "Ms. Drew," Dr. Fell said. "Thank you so much for bringing the files. I understand you suggested the addition of Stafford Bellamy."

Dr. Gabriel Fell was a heavyset man with

white hair. At first glance, he looked like a jolly grandfather, but Nancy noticed that his eyes were more than just old and wise. Nancy guessed that Dr. Fell had seen death in all its most painful forms—and all too often. Somehow, that showed even as he smiled and took Nancy's envelopes.

"The doc likes sitting in the sun too much to pick up his own packages," Varenza teased. "Won't make house calls, either. That goes back to his coroner days. Once, while examining a body at a crime scene, he found the murderer hiding in a closet."

Fell waved the artist away. "I'm sure the young woman has no interest in that old story." He pointed to another chair at the table. "Why don't you sit down while I try to see what story these files might tell."

He opened the folder from Philadelphia first. Sifting through the papers inside, he took a glance at some photos but didn't show them to Nancy. "The crime scene—and the guest of honor," he said briefly. "It's different from what you see on TV and in the movies." He placed the photos facedown. "Unless you want to—"

"No, that's okay," Nancy quickly said.

"You're getting soft, Doc," Varenza accused. "Last time you came to lunch, you had a slide show of people who'd been blown up by bombs."

"I figure it's all part of your job," Dr. Fell said.

"But Ms. Drew doesn't have to look at this mess."

He continued to flip through the papers. "Death was caused by a single wound—a stab to the heart. So the killer was organized . . ."

"Organized?" Nancy echoed.

Fell looked up. "A bit of psychological jargon from our police friends. An organized murderer is in control, he's got a plan. One stab was enough to kill someone—as opposed to chopping the victim into hamburger."

He read on. "Finger bruises on the neck and front of throat. Fractured windpipe, and a broken hyoid bone—that's the U-shaped bone at the base of your tongue. Nice character. He nearly choked this girl to death while he stabbed her. Well, it proves our killer was a strong man. He left the imprint of his hand on Laurel Kenway's throat."

Dr. Fell turned more pages. "The dimensions of the wound matched the knife recovered from Buford Bellamy's car. It was a six-hundred-year-old dagger, a museum piece with a rather distinctive shape. The blade wasn't flat like most knives but was triangular in cross-section."

Fell frowned. "A nasty weapon. It left a wound more like a hole than a simple stab. Blood flowed into the pericardium, the lining around the heart, and also filled the chest cavity. That's what killed the young woman."

"She bled to death?" Nancy said, confused.

"No, the bleeding wasn't that extensive. But the buildup of blood around the heart and lungs made them shut down. To work properly, your heart and lungs need room to expand and contract. But with blood clogging the space around the organs, the victim couldn't draw breath—and her heart couldn't fill with blood to pump."

Nancy shuddered. "How horrible."

Fell shook his head. "No. The horrible thing is the report of cuts on her hands."

"You mean she was slashed trying to protect herself?" Nancy asked.

"No. Those would have been single cuts on the palm of an open hand." Fell demonstrated by raising his hands in a warding-off gesture. Then he picked up a photo. "This shows three parallel slices on the fingers and upper palm."

Nancy thought for a second. "Oh. The knife had three sides."

"Yes. The only way to be cut like that was to hold the blade. That wouldn't have happened before the stabbing. Laurel Kenway either pulled that knife out herself—or more likely, she grabbed the blade as the killer pulled it away. Slipping through her hand, it left those wounds."

Nancy shook her head, trying to push away a wave of sorrow. "She was still fighting, even though she was dead on her feet."

"It's amazing what people can do, despite

being grievously wounded. I've seen people with heart wounds who ran for a block." Fell coughed and changed the subject. "It seems the knife was already at the murder scene. The living room decorations included a shield with the Bellamy crest, with part of an arms and armor collection mounted on the wall."

Fell gave Nancy a bitter smile. "It seems the kind of blade was known as a *misericorde*—a knife built to punch through the plates of a downed knight's armor. If I remember my Latin, the name comes from the word for pity."

He returned to the sheaf of papers. "Body temperature, stomach contents, and the condition of the young woman's muscles—rigor mortis—indicate that death took place between nine-thirty and ten-thirty that night."

The doctor lined up the papers. "All in all, a neat, competent job. No surprises, Ms. Drew."

He went to the next file and spent a few minutes reading before saying to Nancy, "Hmmm. According to this, two other people died in that car crash besides Stafford Bellamy. Hugh and Barbara Owen, the servant staff at the Orbeck mansion. Hugh was the butler/chauffeur, Barbara the maid and cook."

"They were all riding together?" Nancy asked in surprise.

"Not exactly out for a road trip, Ms. Drew," Dr. Fell said as he read on. "Hugh Owen had called 911 for an ambulance. Apparently, Stafford Bellamy was having a heart attack." He frowned. "The only problem with having a private estate is that you're usually out in the middle of nowhere. And, of course, it had to be a dark and stormy night. According to the nephew, Cris Bellamy, who received a call from Owen at the Rittenhouse Square mansion, Owen was told that since Bellamy was conscious, it would be quicker to bring him to the hospital rather than waiting for the EMS ambulance. On the way, they had a head-on collision with a truck."

As Fell continued through the report, he shook his head. "Two lives wasted," he said. "According to the autopsy, Bellamy was dead *before* the crash."

"What?" Nancy stared in disbelief. "How—"

"The medical examiner found that Mr. Bellamy had several broken bones, but there was no vital reaction—no hemorrhage, no bruises, not even swelling around the injury sites. That could only happen because the blood was no longer flowing in Bellamy's body. So what was the cause of death? Ah. A full autopsy showed marked narrowing of the coronary arteries. Bellamy was dead of a heart attack when the limousine hit that truck."

The doorbell rang, and Phil Varenza left his sculpture to answer it. He returned with Frank and Joe Hardy.

"Hey, guys, what are you doing here? You didn't have to get dressed up to come and visit," Nancy said, seeing their shirts and ties. Then she noticed that Joe's hands were filthy, and Frank had a big oil smear across the chest of his white shirt.

"How long ago did you leave Buff Bellamy?" Joe demanded before Nancy had a chance to ask what had happened to them. "And did you notice a car on the estate when you dropped him off?"

"Nice to see you again, too, Joe," Nancy responded angrily. "I'm sure a polite guy like you would like to meet the people you're visiting. Dr. Fell, Mr. Varenza, Frank and Joe Hardy."

"I know Joe sounds a bit short right now," Frank said, "but we just got over a pretty exciting elevator ride."

"Yeah," Joe added. "While we were having lunch with Crispin Bellamy, somebody fiddled with his club's private elevator. We dropped four floors before Frank managed to cut in the emergency brakes. And we had to climb all the way back up a ladder that the fire department put down the shaft. It was an express elevator—no doors on other floors."

He glared at Nancy. "When we finally got out, we checked with Cris Bellamy. He was in a meeting with his boss, but his secretary told us something interesting. She'd gotten a call from

Buff Bellamy. She told him where his brother was having lunch—and that he was talking with us."

Joe's voice was rough as he said to Nancy, "So I found out where you were and came to ask a few questions. Did he have a car? And did he have enough time to get back into town and gimmick that elevator?"

Nancy stared. "You can't be suggesting—"

"Buff was only half an hour away," Joe interrupted angrily. "He knew where we were, and he knows that we—at least, *I*—don't buy this innocence nonsense."

Turning in dismay to Frank, Nancy saw that the older Hardy brother looked as grim as Joe.

"*Somebody* sabotaged the hoist," Frank pointed out. "And the person had to do it just before we left."

"There's something else you ought to know," Joe said. "Before any of this murder stuff, I used to follow Buff's career in the sports magazines. Not only was he a hotshot boat racer—he was right in there with his mechanics. The guy is good with his hands. He knows machinery."

The room seemed to sway around Nancy as she tried to pull her thoughts into order. "No," she said, shaking her head. "It would be stupid for him to do something like that."

"Maybe not so stupid," Joe said. "I'd say he's got you convinced, and even Frank was showing doubts. But Buff knew he hadn't fooled me."

"I didn't see a car out at Orbeck when I dropped Buff off," Nancy argued.

"But that estate is a big place," Joe said. "Are you sure they don't have garages somewhere?"

Nancy had no answer for that.

"Is this a private argument, or can anyone join in?" Dr. Fell inquired with a grin. "Maybe I'm talking outside my specialty—I'm a doctor, not a mechanic." His hand patted the coroner's report on Stafford Bellamy's death. "But it seems we have a case of tampered machinery—as well as an earlier car crash."

"Which could be tampering, too," Nancy admitted. "But where could we find that limo—and could we check it out?"

"You shouldn't doubt Vidocq's resources," the doctor replied. "One of our members is a professional mechanic who specializes in suspicious crashes."

In moments the Hardys were on the phone to Will Resnick, requesting the man's number. "Matt Gerlach," Frank muttered, scribbling on a piece of paper. "And the number at his shop?"

As the boys dialed the mechanic, Nancy wished she could get at a phone and some privacy. In her pocket was the number Buff had given her for his uncle's place in Orbeck. Of course, calling him now would provide no alibi. Too much time had passed since the Hardys' mishap. Buff could have gotten back from town by now.

Frank hung up and reported, "Mr. Gerlach is happy to help us. He's going to check out where the limo wound up, then call us—"

The phone rang. Phil Varenza picked it up, then handed it to Frank.

"Mr. Gerlach? That was fast." Frank listened, then began scribbling again. "Eddie's? Right, right, no, I'm getting the directions down. You'll meet us there in about half an hour? Great! Thanks so much."

He hung up, then turned to the others. "The car was totaled and wound up in a junkyard. Matt Gerlach will meet us there." Frank glanced at Nancy. "Do you want to come with us?"

She shook her head. "I've got a car of my own. Just give me a copy of those directions."

The drive down seemed to match Nancy's mood that day. It started in beautifully kept suburbs but ended in an industrial wasteland. For the last few miles, the landscape had been gray, with what seemed to be hills in the distance. As Nancy came closer, she realized the "hills" were actually huge piles of wrecked cars surrounded by a chain-link fence.

A battered wooden shanty guarded the entrance to the junkyard. As Nancy pulled up and turned off the ignition, she realized the Hardys' battered rental car wasn't around.

"Great," she muttered. "I must have pulled ahead of them and never even noticed. "That ought to make Joe's usual bad mood even better."

In fact, no one was parked at the entrance. Where was Matt Gerlach? she wondered.

Nancy got out of her car and headed for the gate. As she did, a man came hobbling out of the shanty and raised a dirty hand. He could have been as young as forty or as old as seventy, Nancy thought, and he was painfully skinny. To Nancy he looked as much a wreck as some of the dumped cars. "Hold on there, Missy," the man said in a cracked voice. Half his teeth seemed to be missing.

"Are you Eddie?" Nancy asked.

"Me? Eddie?" The man gave a shrill laugh. "The boss got an office in town. I'm the guard."

"I'm waiting for Matt Gerlach," Nancy said. "I guess he must have called."

The man didn't answer; he just stared at her.

"We're supposed to check out a car—the Bellamy limousine. It was in a crash about six months ago."

"Lot Sixteen," the man said. "Got two calls about it, first from some mechanic, then from one of the boys in the office."

He laughed again. "But I think you're too late for checking it out, Missy. They should be putting that sucker in the compactor 'round about now."

Chapter Six

I'M GETTING a whole new look at Nancy Drew," Joe growled as he turned onto the road leading to the junkyard. "She blew right past us without even a wave—in the car *we* rented for her!"

Frank shrugged and patted the worn dashboard of the car they were driving. "She had the better car," he said. "And I guess she had a lot on her mind."

"Like the fact that Buff Bellamy just might be making a fool of her?" Joe's laughter was harsh. "She's not the only one."

"We've got no proof that Buff monkeyed with our elevator," Frank warned.

"Yeah, he just happened to know we were there, and then we took a big drop. That sounds like enough proof to me."

"This investigation isn't supposed to be for you. It's supposed to find a murderer—and to find some concrete evidence." Frank frowned. "I hope this car thing works out. Maybe then we'll have something solid to work with."

"Yeah—unless it annoys your girlfriend or her father." Joe couldn't keep the anger out of his voice. "Then it'll get thrown out of court."

"She's *not* my girlfriend," Frank said sharply. "She's my friend—yours too, unless you keep up this attitude. You know that if Nancy found proof that Buff was guilty, she'd give him up."

"Right, and make her father look like a jerk."

"She'd do the right thing," Frank insisted. "Which I hope you would do if you found something that might help Buff—" He broke off. "There's Nancy's car. But where is she?"

"Probably out fighting with the junkyard dogs," Joe muttered, pulling up beside the other car and stopping. "Poor dogs."

Frank rolled his eyes and got out of the car. He called to a tall, skinny man standing at the junkyard entrance. "Have you seen—"

"Crazy girl!" the guard complained, his voice almost a whine. "Blew up when I told her the car she wanted was goin' to the compactor. Just ran in there like a wild woman!"

Frank didn't even look at Joe. He dashed through the entrance, disappearing down a lane between mounds of junked cars.

As Joe climbed out, he spotted a heavy pickup

truck coming down the road to the junkyard. The truck pulled up behind his car, and a square-faced, chunky man swung down from the cab. "Frank Hardy? Matt Gerlach."

"I'm Joe Hardy. My brother's gone inside already. We may have some trouble."

Gerlach took a moment to question the guard, then hustled inside. "The compactor isn't far inside the yard. That way, it's easier to load the scrap metal—"

His words were interrupted by a female cry and what sounded like the revving of an engine. Joe and the mechanic broke into a run. They swept around one of the mounds of rusting cars to find a narrow lane cutting off to the left. "This is the quickest way to the compactor," Gerlach said.

Unfortunately, the way was also blocked by a filthy forklift. The operator was attempting to pile new stock onto a towering heap of car radiators. Nancy was trying to dart past the utility truck, but the forklift operator kept jockeying his vehicle to block her way.

"Let me by!" Nancy shouted.

"When I finish my job!" the operator retorted with a nasty grin.

Frank Hardy came pounding up behind Joe and Gerlach. Apparently, he'd had to retrace his steps to find the disturbance. When he saw the holdup, he pushed past his brother and the mechanic. "Move that heap—now!"

"You going to make me, boy?" the driver jeered.

Frank hauled himself up onto the machine until he was level with the man at the controls. "I can make a good try," he said flatly. Then he pointed a thumb over his shoulder. "And I have friends to help."

They locked eyes for a long moment. Then the forklift operator glanced away. "Gimme a minute," he muttered.

Frank jumped down, and the driver steered the vehicle to one side, leaving just enough space to pass. Before the forklift even stopped, Nancy was dashing past. Frank, Joe, and Matt Gerlach followed.

"Straight ahead for two mounds, then hang a right," Gerlach shouted. "You'll see the compactor from there!"

Nancy, from her place in the lead, had already reached the intersection. She yelled, pointed, and ran off to the right.

As Joe came closer, he could hear the whine of a high-powered compressor, the shriek of crumpling metal. He reached the turnoff to see Frank and Nancy angrily gesturing at the compactor, arguing with the operator.

"Were we in time?" Gerlach asked.

Nancy turned, her face a mask of fury and frustration. "It's right there," she said, pointing. The pneumatic ramming arm of the compressor pulled away to reveal a cube of metal.

"That's the limousine that Stafford Bellamy died in," Nancy said. "How many clues do you think we'll find in it now?"

The mood in Will Resnick's office was not happy as the Hardys and Nancy reported their discoveries—and their latest setback. Matt Gerlach hadn't accompanied them. As he'd said, "There was nothing for me to do, so there's nothing for me to talk about."

Joe Hardy wanted to talk, if only to point out that Buff Bellamy had once again pulled into the front-runner's place as a suspect. But he didn't want to interrupt Will Resnick's thoughtful silence.

"While you two rushed off to talk to Nancy, Ed Fitzgibbon came over here," Resnick finally said. "He gave me a progress report."

"Or lack of progress," Joe grumbled.

"We've had cases with problems before," Resnick said. "Murders where the victims' families managed to antagonize the police who were supposed to do the investigation." He shook his head. "We even had a case where a murdered kid's parents accused the police of being corrupt."

Resnick leaned back behind his desk. "But I've never seen a case with so many leaks. First, somebody talks to the press. That sets off Gwen Bellamy and causes a media circus around Buff's hotel." He glanced at Nancy. "Nice handling on that, by the way."

"It's the only thing that went right today," she replied.

"Then we've got the tampering with the elevator and the disaster at the junkyard," Resnick went on. "Both of those could have been the result of tipoffs."

Joe was about to name his favorite candidate as to who had given the tips, but Resnick was still speaking.

"While you were driving back, Matt Gerlach gave me a call and sketched out what happened in the junkyard. So we got a jump on that. We tracked down the guy in Eddie Hackett's garbage empire who'd given the order to destroy the car. Turns out we've got a whiff of OC."

"OC?" Nancy repeated.

"Organized crime," Frank translated, but he looked as blank as Nancy. "How do they fit into this?"

"That's what I've been wondering," Resnick said. "It opens a whole new can of worms. But it also offers some interesting possibilities—especially when it comes to news getting around. Our decision to investigate the Bellamy case was made in a dining room, and you questioned Cris Bellamy in a dining room."

"So?" Joe was completely lost.

"One of our local restaurant unions was put under Federal receivership—because of organized crime connections," Resnick said. "That's not to say that all restaurant workers are crooks." He grinned. "Maybe OC types just like to hang out in restaurants." His face grew more serious. "But it shows a possibility as to how the leaks and tipoffs might have occurred."

"Let me get this straight," Joe said. "You're suggesting that a bunch of wiseguys just decided to screw up our investigation?"

"Think of it from the wiseguys' point of view," Frank suddenly said. "You're serving lunch to a roomful of cops and feds, and you hear about this investigation—what a joke!"

"Oh, it may not be a joke," Resnick warned. "Think of what else happened today—evidence destroyed in a junkyard. Bring anything to mind?"

"Auto parts," Frank said quickly. "Stolen cars—chop shops."

"The owner of Eddie's junkyard doesn't have any involvement in such activities. At least, not that we're aware of," Resnick said. "But some of his associates do have connections."

"And the whole result was to stop us from getting a look at the limousine where Stafford Bellamy died." Frank looked impressed. "This could be bigger than we thought."

"It would mean *three* murders, considering what Nancy just told us," Resnick pointed out. "Hugh Owen and his wife, Barbara, died with Bellamy in that car accident—if it was an accident. Bellamy might have been the intended victim, but according to the autopsy reports, his cause of death was a heart attack. And then there's Laurel Kenway."

"Wait a minute." Joe's voice was almost desperate. "You're building a whole theory on a little hot air—these leaks. What would Stafford Bellamy have to do with organized crime?"

"He was in real estate—which means construction," Frank said. "Mobsters have been known to get involved there."

"There are two main motives for murder," Resnick said thoughtfully. "Love and money. According to police investigations, Laurel Kenway wasn't dating anyone when she was murdered. Maybe we should look into the Bellamy money—and Stafford Bellamy's business."

Joe couldn't hold back any longer. "Or maybe we should forget fancy theories and concentrate on where we've got firm evidence. Nothing that's happened in the last two days has cleared Buff Bellamy. *He* could be the one fouling us up. His own sister thinks he's guilty!"

"That does it!" Nancy exploded. She glared at Joe. "I didn't say anything when you kept on making sarcastic remarks. I thought you might come around. But," she continued angrily, "it's obvious that you aren't giving a hundred percent on this case—and aren't going to!"

"Oh, I'm giving a hundred percent," Joe shot back. "You just don't like where I'm giving it."

Nancy turned to Resnick. "Do you think he's right to go after Buff?"

The Vidocq commissioner shrugged. "I think investigators should go where their gut feelings send them. Even when a person is wrong, that kind of work clears the underbrush. Sometimes it even helps to strengthen the real case."

"I don't disagree with that," Nancy said. "What I don't like is the way Joe makes himself blind to anything that even *suggests* Buff might be innocent."

"I'm not blind—there's nothing to see," Joe retorted.

"Nothing to see? Let's ignore this whole organized crime theory for a second. Instead, I'll just ask about Buff's family. Did his sister even talk to you? Did his brother really tell you anything? From what I heard, he was pretty evasive when Mr. Fitzgibbon began asking questions."

"Probably trying to keep his brother from being hanged," Joe insisted.

"Oh? Can you back that up with facts? Or should I just take it as fact because the Great Joe said so?" Nancy squared off against him. "I thought it was only fair to ask you in on this investigation. But I'm really tired of getting too little, too late—not to mention all these leaks."

"So what are you going to do about it?" Joe couldn't keep the taunting tone out of his voice.

"I'm going to follow up on one angle—

another way of looking at what Mr. Resnick just said."

Nancy glanced toward the head of the Vidocq Society. "You suggested that murders are committed for love or money. Stafford Bellamy had millions, so there's another motive to consider—who inherits?"

Joe opened his mouth to point out the obvious—Buff Bellamy was one of the heirs. But Nancy rushed on before he could speak. "We need a good look at the Bellamys, and I'm sorry, Mr. Resnick, we can't do it hands-off. So I'd like to do it close up and personal . . ."

Joe almost flinched as Nancy glared at him. "And alone!"

Chapter Seven

FRANK HARDY WATCHED unhappily as Nancy stormed out of the office. Then he glanced at Will Resnick, who only shrugged. "That's the last time I'll say an investigator should follow gut feelings," the Vidocq commissioner said. "She followed hers right out of the office."

Joe, however, looked pleased to see Nancy leave. "Well, now that we've got the prima donna off the team, maybe we can get down to work and finish this up."

"Finish off Buff Bellamy, you mean." Frank gave his brother a hard look.

Joe blinked in surprise. "Ah, come on. I figured with Nancy gone, you'd—"

"I'd go along with you?" Frank finished for his brother. "Too bad. I think it might be a good idea for someone on the team to work in a leak-free environment. There's just too much on this case that doesn't add up."

"Now that Miss Poor-Buff-Is-Innocent is gone, I can speak my mind," Joe said. "This is an open-and-shut case. Think about it. What was the one part of Buff's lie detector test that he failed? The question about whether he'd fought with Laurel. They were about the same age. Maybe they had a relationship or something and had a fight. He got angry, things got out of control, and he killed her."

"But Buff passed the polygraph when he denied killing Laurel," Frank pointed out.

Joe waved the point away. "I've been thinking about that," he said. "And maybe I've figured it out. Bellamy prepared himself somehow to answer that murder question, so he passed the lie detector. But he wasn't set up for that question about just fighting with Laurel, so there was a reaction."

Frank's eyebrows rose. "That's your theory?"

"Yes, and it fits the facts," Joe said defensively.

"Not all of them," Frank responded. "The crime scene doesn't seem to bear out your theory." He glanced at Will Resnick. "Would you say so?"

The Customs man shook his head. "Not from what I heard from Dr. Fell—and saw in the coroner's report. Laurel Kenway died of a single stab wound," he said. "That would seem to point to a more cold-blooded murder." Resnick looked grim. "In my experience, angry killers make something of a mess. They stab more than once. They may even slash the victim. And," he added, "as I said earlier, when Laurel died she wasn't seeing anyone."

"So Nancy may be right," Frank suggested. "Instead of looking at love, we should look to the money for a motive."

"Fine—fine," Joe surrendered. "We'll keep looking." He sighed. "And I guess that Nancy will be looking, too—whatever her plan might be."

As soon as Nancy was back in her hotel room, she dug out the number for the Bellamy mansion in Orbeck. Buff answered on the third ring.

"Boy, am I glad to hear a friendly voice," he said.

"From what I hear, you've been on the phone enough," Nancy replied.

"Well, I called Cris to tell him I was here. He was out of the office, but when he called back, we almost had a fight. Cris doesn't think it's a good idea for me to stay—not with Gwen living here, too."

"I thought she had moved to the mansion in town."

"No, she was just meeting people there." Buff sighed. "Something about her wedding plans, Cris tells me. The town house has pretty much been empty since Laurel was killed. Sometimes Cris crashes there when he works really late at the office. But even he prefers to commute from Orbeck."

Buff gave a nervous laugh. "Cris says he'll try to get home before Gwen and act as referee."

"Well, I hope there's room for another house guest," Nancy said. "Because I'm coming out there, too."

"To stay?" Buff blurted out. "I mean—well, Cris told me Gwen was pretty nasty to the Vidocq investigators who tried to question her."

"So we won't tell anyone that I'm an investigator," Nancy said. "It's called going undercover."

"Then how do I explain—" Buff began.

"Buff," Nancy said as patiently as she could. "You're a guy, I'm a girl. Does that suggest something we could pretend to be?"

For a second there was dead silence over the phone. "You're coming here pretending to be my girlfriend?" Buff finally said. "Oh, Gwen is just going to *love* this."

Nancy ignored the worried tone in his voice. "We'll have to come up with a cover story—where I come from, how we met. The best thing is to use a large helping of truth and a little fibbing. We can say I come from a small town near Chicago, but not mention River Heights. Now, where could we have met?"

"Hey, a lot of Midwest girls come down to Florida for spring break," Buff said. "When I was racing down there, babes always came around—ah, I mean—"

"Spring break it is," Nancy said. "That should do. We don't want to get too fancy." She glanced at her watch. "I'll be there in about an hour."

Nancy hung up the phone and quickly packed some clothes into a bag, which she put beside Buff's two suitcases. Then she changed into a nutmeg-colored miniskirt with a matching V-neck jacket, and a white silk T-shirt. A plain blouse and black skirt were fine for impersonating a waitress and delivering files. But playing a girlfriend required something a little more stylish. Luckily, Nancy had planned on visiting her aunt in New York after going to the Vidocq Society meeting, so she had a choice of clothes.

Not long afterward, Nancy drove her rental car between a pair of gray stone gateposts and down a gravel drive toward the Bellamy mansion. There were muddy spots in the drive, and the lawn was shaggy, but the hundred-year-old house was still impressive as she approached it. The walls were of gray stone and the roof of reddish tile. Thick brick chimneys poked into the sky, and there was even a round turret at one corner. How could one family have lived in such a sprawling place? Nancy wondered as she brought the car to a halt.

Buff appeared at the front door—he must have been watching for her. Nancy bounced out of the car, flung her arms around him, and gave him a big kiss.

"Um—you don't have to. There's nobody home," Buff said.

"It's better to keep up the act rather than forget it at the wrong time." Nancy glanced at the windows. "I figured there might be servants around."

"Not anymore," Buff said. "My uncle only had two servants living in, and they were the ones who also died in the car crash. With the will still up in the air, there's not much money. Gwen has a housekeeper in during the day, but she just finished up." He gave Nancy a look. "She was kind of annoyed about the extra people for dinner."

"I guess we'll have to do some shopping," Nancy said. "Now, we have some more stuff to get straight. You can't call me Nancy Drew, because everybody knows my father defended you. It would be easier if my alias sounded something like my name. How about Mandy? Mandy . . . Dean."

"Okay," Buff said. "Mandy Dean it is." They took the bags out of the car and headed inside, up a flight of stairs, then down a long hall. "I tried to pick out a decent guest bedroom." Buff stopped in front of a heavy mahogany door. "Sorry if it's a little stuffy. My uncle wasn't one for entertaining."

It was a good-size room, but the furniture was large and old-fashioned. Nancy opened the window wider. "I made up the bed," Buff said, sounding almost shy. "And I left towels and stuff. There's a connecting bathroom."

Nancy grinned. "The society host with the personal touch."

Buff shook his head. "My family may have a grand old name—we were in Philadelphia before the Revolutionary War—but my parents weren't rolling in dough. Uncle Stafford was definitely our rich relative."

"And he didn't have a family of his own?" Nancy asked as she unpacked.

Buff shrugged. "He never married—too busy building up his company or something. But he always had the three of us over—Gwen, Cris, and myself. And, of course, there was Laurel. She was the daughter of my uncle's business partner. Her mother died when she was only a year old. Then, when she was six or seven, her father died, and she came to live with my uncle. I know this seems unbelievable, but a few years later, my parents died, so Gwen, Cris, and I wound up here, too—although my uncle sent us to boarding school, so we weren't around much."

"How did your parents die?" Nancy asked.

"My dad overworked himself," Buff said. "He was a lawyer, sort of a family advisor for the old first families. Then all these big, high-powered law firms began moving into town. My dad tried to compete with them and wound up dying of a heart attack. I don't think my mother ever got over the shock. She passed away less than a year after my dad died."

"So your dad didn't make a lot of money then," Nancy said.

"No," Buff responded. "We were always Bellamys, and the name means something in this town. There are a lot of families like us—social but not rich." Buff jammed his hands into his pockets. "With Uncle Stafford, though, we became something else—heirs."

He glanced at Nancy. "I don't think it's a good thing, expecting to inherit money. Gwen's turned into more and more of a snob, waiting to inherit all this money. I went into boat racing, won a little, lost a little—and wound up in debt. Maybe Cris had the best idea, going into the family business. But I couldn't do that."

"Everybody knew about your uncle's will?" Nancy asked.

"I suppose so," Buff replied. "Uncle Stafford used my father's firm to draw up the will, even though my dad had passed away. With less and less business, it's really a one-man office now—Dad's former partner, Wallace Collingwood, ran it from his house."

He shook his head. "In fact, we almost didn't have a will to fight over. We couldn't find it. Mr. Collingwood had a stroke and was in the hospital when my uncle died. His home office was a mess.

Cris finally turned up a copy of the will in some of Uncle Stafford's personal papers."

"And that's when the trouble began," Nancy said.

Buff's shoulders slumped. "No. The trouble began when I got arrested. The will was pretty straightforward. There were donations to charities and so on. Laurel was supposed to receive a small trust fund. But most of my uncle's estate was to be divided three ways—among Gwen, Cris, and myself."

"You don't think Laurel's inheritance had any connection with her death?" Nancy asked.

"Compared to what the three of us are supposed to get, the trust fund is chicken feed." Buff's face tightened. "Not that we've seen anything. Gwen tied up the whole inheritance process with her lawsuit against me."

"She's really suing to keep you out of the inheritance?"

Buff's voice was very low. "She really believes I'm a murderer. And she's determined that I'm not going to get any of the estate."

The sound of a car engine came through the open window.

"That may be Gwen now," Buff said. "Come on downstairs. Maybe when you see her, you'll understand."

At least I'll understand what I'm up against, Nancy thought as she followed Buff into the hallway.

"I've got you on the other side of the house from her room." Buff gestured toward another hallway. "Gwen has the turret room. Being the oldest, she got first choice."

They came down the stairs to find a young man who looked like an older version of Buff standing in the entrance hall. Nancy realized this had to be Cris Bellamy. "I tried to get home before—" He stopped speaking as he saw Nancy.

"Mandy Dean, this is my brother, Cris," Buff said as he reached the ground. "Mandy is a—er, *friend* of mine. She'll be staying for a few days."

"Oh," Cris said, still staring up at Nancy. "You hadn't mentioned you were bringing a guest." Cris shot a look at his younger brother. Nancy translated it as, *Have you gone out of your mind?*

"This is my home, too, isn't it?" Buff asked.

"Yes—yes, of course it is," Cris answered. Even so, he looked worried. And he looked even more worried as the door front opened and Gwen Bellamy walked in, accompanied by a slim young man.

Nancy was still standing on the stairs, and at first Gwen didn't see her. But Nancy could see the young woman's reaction to Buff. Gwen stopped and stared, a look of shock on her face.

Then Gwen caught a glimpse of Nancy. She didn't say anything, but she glared at the intruder.

Cris Bellamy spoke up, making nervous introductions. "Uh, Gwen, this is Mandy Dean, a friend of Buff's. Mandy, my sister, Gwen, and her fiancé, Lawrence Harleigh."

"Hi," Nancy said, trying to put a bit of airhead in her voice. "Nice to meet you."

Gwen Bellamy said nothing.

"Are you from Philadelphia?" Lawrence Harleigh asked.

Nancy went right into the cover story she'd worked up with Buff. "Nah. I'm from the Midwest, originally. First time I saw the ocean was when I went on spring break last year in Florida." She glanced at Buff. "That's where I met this guy racing his boat."

"I think I'll go see what's been prepared for supper," Gwen said, her tone cold.

"The housekeeper said she'd leave something to take care of all of us," Buff said.

"Want some help?" Nancy offered brightly.

Gwen speared her with a look. "I'm sure I can manage. Want to come along, Lawrence?"

It wasn't really a question. Lawrence followed in silence as Gwen headed off for a part of the house Nancy hadn't seen yet.

Cris waited until they were out of earshot before he spoke. "So . . . has Buff given you the guided tour?"

"Not yet," Nancy replied. "But why don't you guys hang out for a while? I wouldn't mind washing up—and I'm sure you have a lot to talk about."

She headed back up the stairs. But she didn't go to her room. Instead, she followed the hallway Buff had pointed to. Nancy knew that it led to the turret room, Gwen Bellamy's private quarters.

Her Highness should be busy in the kitchen for a while, Nancy thought. Maybe I can find something that might explain why she's so hot to cut Buff out of the inheritance.

The door was unlocked. Nancy eased it open and slipped inside. She found herself in a large, beautifully decorated space. Although the wall near the door was flat, the room was almost circular. The walls were painted a pale violet, which matched the tapestry covers on the canopy bed and the drapes flanking the two windows. The furniture was mahogany, including two huge wardrobes that served as closets. The room even had a small fireplace, with antique bronze figurines on the mantel.

Nancy was heading for the desk, which was set against one of the windows, when she heard muffled voices in the hallway. She froze. Could it be Cris and Buff heading to their rooms?

No. That was a female voice, and it was coming closer! The doorknob rattled, and Nancy flung herself toward the nearest hiding place as the door opened.

Chapter Eight

"CAN YOU BELIEVE that girl?" Gwen Bellamy demanded as Nancy crouched against the side of a wardrobe, concealed by the canopy hangings of the four-poster bed. It wasn't the best hideout in that room, only the closest. She couldn't be seen from the doorway and could always slip under the bed if Gwen came deeper into the room.

Luckily, the eldest of the Bellamy heirs stalked back and forth by the door. "It's not enough that Buff comes waltzing back here, he brings that—that—"

"That girl named Mandy Dean," Lawrence Harleigh finished up for her. "Rather pretty, I thought."

Gwen's pacing abruptly stopped. "Oh, do you? Well, she looked very low-class to me. And why would any girl—pretty or otherwise—hook herself up with a murderer? I can only think of two reasons. The most obvious is that she's a gold digger. This Dean girl hopes to get a piece of Buff's inheritance."

"I sort of guessed that myself," Lawrence said. "What's your other theory?"

Gwen's voice was filled with disgust. "The only sort of person who'd get involved with a killer would have to be the same kind."

"Oh, so Mandy is a killer, too?" Lawrence asked.

That shut Gwen up for a moment. "Perhaps that's going too far," she finally admitted. "But I'm sure she's some kind of criminal. For all we know, she's here to—what do thieves call it?—case the joint.' "

"Oh, come on, Gwen," Lawrence said.

"This is even worse than his last serious romance," Gwen went on. "Heaven knows, *that* caused enough problems."

Nancy almost leaned out of her hiding place when she heard these words. She wished she could have seen Gwen's face as she spoke.

There was no hope of that, though. All Nancy could do was crouch against the wall of the wardrobe and strain to hear.

Unfortunately, Gwen didn't discuss Buff. She went on to complain about her other brother. "At least then we dealt with the problem as a family. But now we can't depend on Cris at all.

He's bending over backward to make nice with Buff and that bimbo. Useless!"

"So what are we supposed to do with the evil Mandy?" Lawrence asked. "Shall I track her down and push her off the roof?"

Gwen laughed for a moment, then said, "Would you?"

"Hey, honey, I'm a lawyer," Lawrence responded. "The first stuff we learn about is self-incrimination. That means if I were going to kill someone, I'm not supposed to talk about it."

"Right," Gwen said. "So, would you?"

He chuckled. "No comment."

A long moment of silence followed, then came a lip-smacking noise. Nancy realized with embarrassment that the couple must be kissing.

"I suppose I'd better go look at that food," Gwen finally said with a sigh.

"You should have let Mandy take care of it," Lawrence said with a laugh.

"I don't want to worry about her poisoning us," Gwen grumbled. But there was a bubble of laughter in her voice, too.

"If your uncle's will had been probated," Lawrence said, "you'd inherit your share of his money. You could afford some servants to take care of this big old barn. At least you could have a full-time cook—"

Gwen's good humor vanished in an instant. "That will isn't going to be probated until Buff's been cut out," she flared. "I'll make sure he doesn't get his hands on a penny!"

"You want my professional opinion on that?" Lawrence asked.

"No," she replied. "I have to *try,* don't you see? It's the least I can do for poor Laurel." Nancy could hear what sounded like guilt in Gwen's voice.

"Hiring detectives, starting a family feud—it's a shame you weren't so concerned for her when she was alive," Lawrence said cuttingly.

Nancy expected Gwen Bellamy to explode. Instead, there was just an uncomfortable silence. At last, Lawrence finally said, "We'd better get downstairs and into the kitchen."

They left, but Nancy counted off ten seconds before she finally peeked around the side of the wardrobe. The room was empty. She quickly headed for the door but froze with her hand on the knob. How long would it take for the couple to reach the stairs and descend out of sight?

A minute passed, but it felt more like an eternity. Nancy no longer wanted to search the room, she wanted to get out of there. The couple she'd eavesdropped on had left her with a lot to think about. Gwen was obviously an awful snob, and she had a bad temper, too. Lawrence seemed a twisty character, with his jokes about murder. He seemed very interested in Gwen's inheritance, too. But Lawrence had also shown some interest in Mandy Dean. Maybe a little flirting would get him to open up. . . .

Deciding that the couple had to be far enough away by now, Nancy yanked open the door, dashed into the hallway—and slammed into a broad, muscular chest.

She bounced backward in shock, heart hammering. Should have looked before I leaped, she thought. Only then did she realize she hadn't been caught by any of the people she'd come to investigate. She'd crashed into Buff Bellamy.

"You—you startled me," Nancy finally said when she got her breath back.

"I got bored with Cris and decided to find you to offer the guided tour again," Buff said. "Uncle Stafford was very proud of the house. And, of course, there's always Fort Bellamy."

Nancy gave him a surprised glance. "There's a fort here named after your family?"

Buff laughed. "It's actually the old stables. My uncle was quite the military collector—I'm not going to tell you more. You have to see it for yourself."

He glanced at Gwen's door, now closed behind Nancy's back. "But then, it looks as though you've been looking around on your own."

"Not just looking, but hearing," Nancy said. "I just managed to duck out of view when your sister and her fiancé came in."

Buff shook his head. "Judging from the look

on her face downstairs, I bet you got an earful." He glanced at her. "Who was she talking about?"

"Oh, your brother. And, of course, me."

He rolled his eyes. "Yeah. I'm sure she just *loves* having you here."

"Well, it's the first time I ever heard anyone call me a bimbo."

Buff flushed. "You've got to understand about Gwen. You see, she's—"

"She's a real snob," Nancy finished. "By the way, she considers me even worse than your last 'serious romance.' What was *that* all about?"

Even as the joking words left her mouth, Nancy saw a change came over Buff. He had struck her as big and strong, the perfect, easygoing jock. His smile and youthful enthusiasm made Nancy think of a large, healthy, *friendly* animal. Seeing Buff now was like watching a big teddy bear suddenly transform into a snarling grizzly.

Buff stared at her, his eyes about as warm as a pair of blue stones in a frozen stream bed. "That has nothing to do with this case," he said, his voice low and cold. "Nothing."

Buff stepped forward, looming over Nancy. Instinctively she took a step back and realized she was pinned against the door. "So why don't you just forget you ever heard Gwen mention that?" Buff continued. "It will be better all around."

"Okay, if that's the way you'd like it." If Nancy's voice was soft and soothing, her eyes were sharp as she studied Buff's face. "I didn't mean to hit a nerve."

Buff stepped back to let Nancy pass. She saw he still had to fight to keep his face blank. "It's not that," he began. "It's just—personal."

Nancy decided it would be better to let Buff cool down before they talked any more. "I—uh, think I'll just go for a walk before dinner. Okay?"

Buff shrugged, not even turning as Nancy started down the hallway. "Suit yourself. Just listen for the dinner bell. In nice weather, we usually have dinner on the patio in the rear of the house."

Nancy headed down the hall to the stairway. No one was around on the first floor, so she crossed the foyer and went out the door.

Gravel crunched under her feet as Nancy followed the circular drive. Then she stepped off the path and onto the front lawn. A moment later she was passing the window of what had to be the main living room. A grin appeared on Nancy's face. In a way, Gwen had been right. She *was* casing the joint.

Overgrown grass stalks whipped against Nancy's shins almost to her knees as she moved on. If Buff wants to get on Gwen's good side, maybe I should suggest that he mow this stuff, she thought.

But as Nancy reached the tower room at the

corner of the house, her good humor faded. It seemed as if Gwen's bad temper ran in the family, judging from the way Buff's usual good nature had cracked. She shivered a little. The only way to describe Buff's outburst upstairs was . . . scary.

Could he have killed Laurel Kenway—maybe as the result of an argument? Nancy pushed the idea away. There were other suspects she wanted to think about.

Gwen certainly had a shorter fuse. Suppose her talk about "poor Laurel" and insistence on Buff's guilt was some sort of an act? And then there was the clever fiancé. Nancy knew from watching her father at work that lawyers sometimes had to be good actors. The question was, how good was Lawrence Harleigh?

Nancy's steps slowed in the tangled grass as she replayed the conversation she'd overheard. Yes, she'd say Lawrence was smart. And she couldn't get over the way he'd brought up the subject of murder, even if it had been a joke.

Another point struck her. Lawrence seemed to have an eye for pretty girls. And judging from her pictures in the paper, Laurel Kenway had been very pretty. Had he perhaps gotten involved with Laurel—until she became a hindrance to his plans to marry the Bellamy heiress?

And then there was hotheaded Gwen. What would she do if she discovered her fiancé was fooling around? And with a girl she considered little more than a charity case whom her uncle had taken in?

Nancy could easily imagine an argument between the two young women. All it would take was one blow struck in anger. A fatal blow . . .

Her thoughts were interrupted by the vigorous ringing of the dinner bell. Whoever was ringing it must have good arms, Nancy thought. But then, there's a lot of ground to cover.

Nancy realized she, too, had a bit of ground to cover if she was going to circle the house. She picked up her pace and rounded another corner, only to find a new wing of the mansion in her way. When she got around that, she saw several outbuildings.

She saw Cris Bellamy coming out of a long, ramshackle pile of a place. The old stables, Nancy thought. It was just far enough away to keep horsy smells from disturbing people in the house.

Buff's older brother smiled and waved as Nancy came into view from behind the base of one of the huge chimneys. Then Nancy's attention shifted to a creaking noise above her.

She looked up just in time to see the chimney disintegrate into a cascade of bricks—all falling straight at her!

Chapter Nine

IN HIS HOTEL ROOM, Frank Hardy picked up the phone and dialed Will Resnick's office. When the Special Agent answered, Frank said, "Maybe I'm wasting your time, but I just can't forget what you told Nancy about money being a motive for murder. She's checking out the Bellamy family finances. But suppose the motive comes from the Bellamy business interests?"

"You mean the organized crime connection?" Resnick sounded dubious. "That might explain someone killing the old man. But there's no connection to the murder of Laurel Kenway."

"Just a long shot," Frank apologized.

Surprisingly, Resnick chuckled. "It's a long shot we've started looking into. A couple of our people—agents from the FBI and IRS—are going to the Bellamy offices to sniff around. Want to go along with them?"

"Would we?" Frank burst out.

After hanging up the phone, he rousted Joe, who was napping. "Ties back on," he announced. "We're talking to business people and have to dress for success."

They rushed to the futuristic spire that housed the offices of Bellamy Holdings. The area of new commercial buildings was only minutes from Rittenhouse Square, yet seemed centuries away. In spite of the narrow streets, these structures of glass and steel looked like something out of a science fiction movie.

Two men waited for them in the building's chrome and neon lobby. "I take it you're the Hardys," a big, bulky man with rimless glasses and thinning black hair said. "I'm Steve Portino."

"*You're* the FBI guy?" Joe blurted.

"Please forgive my kid brother," Frank said, giving Joe a murderous look. "I think he's trying to set a new world's record: How many times in one case he can put his foot in his mouth."

"Too many movies." Portino's chubby face lit up with a grin. "The fact is, the Bureau targets lawyers and accountants for recruiting." He brushed a hand over the lapel of his slightly too-tight suit jacket. "Which do I look like?"

"Pretty obvious, I guess." If Frank opened a dictionary, he'd expect to see Portino's picture next to the definition of "accountant." The pocket of the heavyset man's white shirt bulged with pens and pencils. His jacket slanted to one side from the weight of a pocket calculator. And the knot of his tie was askew and had shrunk to the size of a peanut.

If anything, Frank would have picked Portino's companion as the FBI man—slim, with intense blue eyes and a blond crew cut. The man thrust out a hand. "Rick Sharpe," he identified himself. "IRS."

"Internal Revenue Service," Frank said.

"More commonly known as the tax man." Portino nudged his companion. "A pair of nice young guys like you are just what we need to soften these people up while we probe their numbers."

They took the elevator up to Bellamy Holdings. As Frank got off the elevator in this ultramodern building, he felt as if he were entering an eighteenth-century mansion. The walls were hand-carved dark mahogany panels, and a huge antique desk dominated the reception area. A stunning young woman sitting behind the desk greeted them.

Frank didn't know which three letters were responsible—FBI or IRS—or all six together. But the effect on the Bellamy offices was almost magical. A distinguished-looking gray-haired man in an expensive suit came out to greet them as soon as they arrived.

"I'm Richard Tacey, executive vice-president. Stafford Bellamy was our president, but with his death, I'm running things."

"We're sorry to be bothering you so late in the business day," Frank said.

Joe glanced around. "I sort of expected to be dealing with Cris Bellamy."

"Ah, Crispin left early," Tacey replied. "I've put his office at your disposal." The executive turned to the receptionist, who stood with a tall stack of papers in her arms. "Here are our financial statements for the last ten years. I'm sure you'll find them pretty straightforward."

Sharpe laughed. "With a company this size, *no* finances are straightforward."

Tacey's face tightened. "Our records are checked by one of the country's top accounting firms." He sounded angry, but Frank saw a sheen of sweat on his forehead. "Are you suggesting—"

"I'm suggesting that this is a large company, with a lot of money and a lot of projects." Sharpe cut Tacey off. "You can't report on that without getting complicated."

The executive showed them to the office in frosty silence. When the door closed, Frank turned to Sharpe with raised eyebrows. "Is it just me, or does that guy seem nervous?"

"It's a hazard of the job," Portino said. "Talking to the IRS makes anybody nervous."

An hour or so passed, with the Hardys just

sitting around as the Vidocq Society's financial experts sorted through the records.

"Maybe I was wrong," Sharpe finally admitted. "Accountants are supposed to be conservative. But these guys are bending over backward when it comes to their books." He shook his head. "They're not even using tricks they could get away with—and it's cost them money."

"Well, it looks like we're not going to find anything in this stuff—at least, not in the last ten years." Portino stood up and stretched. "We're going to keep at it, though. But you guys can help out."

He scribbled a telephone number on a sheet of paper and passed it to Frank. "This is the phone in room three-seventeen—the press room at police headquarters. Ask for Art Farnsworth. He's a crime reporter, and a member of the society. I'm hoping he can put you in touch with a financial reporter who can tell us more about the history of Bellamy Holdings."

Portino consulted a battered plastic notebook, then jotted down another number and gave it to Joe. "This will put you in touch with a guy from the financial section on another paper. We met on a fraud case I investigated a while back. Mention my name and see if he can dig up anything."

The boys quickly headed down to the lobby pay phones and made their calls. Both returned with sheafs of notes. "Your friend in headquarters referred me to an old-timer on the city finance beat," Frank said. "It looks like you called it. Bellamy Holdings is very much on the up-and-up—today. But there are some skeletons in their financial closet—and they date back to more than ten years ago."

"Yeah," Joe chimed in. "Back to the days when the company was a partnership. Bellamy and Kenway. It seems Kenway was accused of fraud. Those were the high points my source remembered. But he gave me a number for the guy who broke the story, a reporter who's retired now—Harry Allison. I called him, and he'll see us right away." He glanced at the investigators, who seemed to be up to their elbows in papers.

"We'll trust you to get the history," Sharpe said.

Allison lived in a shabby building a short cab ride from the center city. His apartment door was opened by a middle-aged woman wearing the white uniform of a nurse's aide. "Are *you* the ones who got Mr. Allison all up in the trees? He's had me digging in his closets, looking for old papers, ever since you called!"

Still complaining, she led them into the living room, where Harry Allison awaited them.

Frank stared. The newspaperman was old and massively heavy. He sat in a worn armchair in pajamas and a heavy robe. The top of his head was as bald as an egg, with whitish gray hair growing in unruly tufts around the sides. He grinned when he saw the boys, revealing a few scattered teeth and throwing a network of wrinkles over his face.

But the blue eyes behind the thick lenses of his glasses were alert and sharp. "Which one of you is Joe Hardy?" he demanded, his throaty voice surprisingly firm.

"I am," Joe said. "This is my brother, Frank."

"So, both Hardy boys," Allison said. "I read about your work in the Kenway murder case."

Frank couldn't help himself. "You did?"

"Listen, boy. I'm old, but I'm not dead yet. I read all the newspapers in this town, and my brain hasn't gotten as bad as my body." Allison coughed from deep in his chest.

"Fifty years I spent covering this town, before I had to retire. Now the paper I worked for doesn't exist anymore." He patted the dusty scrapbook in his lap. "But I've got copies of my stories here."

Allison gave them another gap-toothed grin. "You looked surprised when I mentioned the Laurel Kenway case, but you shouldn't be. I started the investigation that put her father away."

He opened the book. Yellowed newspaper clippings covered each page. As the old reporter flipped along, Frank saw headlines about Bellamy and Kenway, warnings of fraud, then coverage of an investigation and court case.

"When Stafford Bellamy and Walter Kenway

linked up, it seemed like the perfect partnership," Allison explained. "Bellamy had some prime real estate and a bit of money. Kenway was an ambitious builder with a good track record. Working together, they hit the big time."

The old man shook his head. "But real estate has its ups and downs. Build an office building when everybody's buying, and you make a fortune. With the same building in a bad market, you lose your shirt. That's what happened to Bellamy and Kenway. They had a bunch of projects come due right when the market went in the dumper."

Allison shrugged. "Kenway had a reputation as a wheeler-dealer. So it's not surprising he began moving money around, trying to keep those projects from going belly-up. The problem was, *all* the projects were in trouble, so shuffling funds didn't help. Kenway finally got caught, in part thanks to some articles I wrote. By the time he actually went to trial, it turned out that a lot of money had disappeared. People who'd invested in the deals got back only pennies for each dollar they'd put up. A lot of people were financially wiped out—and that included quite a few of Stafford Bellamy's society friends."

"What happened to Kenway?" Frank asked.

The old reporter paged through stories about the fraud trial. "Kenway admitted to trying some creative accounting to save the company but denied that he'd taken money. The guilty verdict just about killed him. Poor guy died in prison, only a couple of months into his sentence. All he had in the way of a family was a daughter, six or seven years old."

"And Stafford Bellamy took her into his house," Joe said. "Pretty generous, considering her father almost put him out of business."

"Society people have their own ideas on doing the right thing," Allison replied. "Bellamy saved his side of the business, and when the market recovered, he went on to make a bundle."

"Which is better than what happened to all those investors." Frank frowned. "I wonder where we could get a list of them?"

"That I can't help you with," Allison said.

"But can we borrow your book?" Joe asked.

"And your phone?" Frank added.

The old reporter was more willing to give up his phone than his scrapbook, but in the end he agreed. The boys called Will Resnick and arranged to meet him at his office. When they arrived, they found a thin, aristocratic-looking man sitting beside the Special Agent's desk.

"Meet Austin White, the society's resident blueblood," Resnick said. "He had the biggest obstacle to becoming a street cop that I ever saw. He belongs to one of the most important society families in the city."

"Then maybe *you* can tell us a little social gossip from about fifteen years ago," Frank said as they shook hands. "I was told a lot of

Philadelphia's first families lost money when Bellamy and Kenway went bust. Do you know any?"

"We could start with my own family," White said. "They invested heavily because they considered Bellamy one of their own kind. Kenway wouldn't have gotten a penny out of them—he started out as a bricklayer, you know."

Frank smiled. "So people were willing to put up their money because they knew and trusted Stafford Bellamy."

"Right," White said. "Bellamy's own family invested. His brother, Bart, went in so heavily he was wiped out."

Bartholomew Bellamy? Frank frowned. That was the father of Gwen, Cris, and Buff. "Anyone else that you know of?"

"Clement Harleigh nearly lost his house when the company crashed," White replied.

"He wouldn't happen to have a son named Lawrence? A lawyer?" Frank asked.

White looked surprised. "His only son. He's engaged to the Bellamy girl."

Joe shook his head. "Interesting as all this might be, it's old news." He chuckled and looked at his brother. "I guess none of this stuff will end up being leaked."

Frank, however, frowned. "Maybe not as old as you think, Joe. The company that ruined all these people—and more—was Bellamy and

Kenway. We have two dead people—a Bellamy and a Kenway."

"You think it's an old grudge?" Resnick asked.

"I don't know," Frank admitted. "But it worries me—because if it's true, the Bellamy heirs may be in danger."

Chapter Ten

NANCY, STARING UP at the bricks, was momentarily paralyzed. Then, as she was about to react, a body slammed into her, and together they seemed to fly through the air.

Bricks thundered down behind her as she landed on the grass. A shocked Nancy found herself wrapped in the arms of Cris Bellamy. "Sorry about being so rough," he said. "I was afraid you weren't going to make it out from under without a running start."

He helped her up.

"You—" Nancy coughed to clear a suddenly tight throat. "You seem awfully calm about a whole chimney falling down."

"It's not exactly a surprise. We all knew the masonry was rotten. Buff should have warned you." Cris looked bitter. "Uncle Stafford was going to have it repaired before he died, and that was almost a year ago. But since Buff's trial, our inheritances have all been tied up by Gwen's court battle. We have no money to keep this place up. We'd have to petition the court executor, and that takes more time than you'd believe."

"Does the house need that much work?" Nancy asked.

He shrugged. "Once a building gets over a hundred years old, you'd be surprised at all the fixing it needs. My salary would be a drop in the bucket. In fact, I'd say this week's pay will go to cleaning up the mess here." Cris gave her a smile. "So don't do your aerobics up in your bedroom. You might wind up dropping through the living room ceiling."

Nancy laughed, but her eyes were serious as she scanned the roof of the mansion. The chimney's collapse might have been an accident, as Cris said. But if everybody in the house knew that it was about to fall, somebody could have helped it along.

"We'd better get to the dinner table," Cris said. "When Gwen rings that bell, she expects everybody to turn up on the double." He glanced at the huge pile of bricks they'd just avoided. "Our only excuse for not showing would be if we were buried under those."

In spite of her narrow escape, Nancy couldn't

help smiling as she followed Cris around to the rear of the Bellamy mansion. Buff hadn't mentioned that his older brother was quite so charming.

At last they came around the wing. Nancy saw that the "patio" Cris and Buff had talked about was a flagstoned area large enough for full-court basketball.

It was a warm spring evening, and a dining table with a shining white cloth stood in the shade of a canopy. An annoyed-looking Gwen stood with a tray at the french doors that led from the house. Only Buff had responded to the call for dinner.

"At least we aren't the last ones," Nancy said. "Lawrence isn't here, either."

"Do you have to ruin my appetite right before dinner?" Cris asked, almost in disgust.

Nancy's eyebrows rose. "It sounds as though you're not fond of your brother-in-law-to-be."

"He's a very dangerous kind of person—an aristocrat who's broke." Cris spoke in a flat voice. "Since he can't inherit, he figures on marrying money. That's easy, he thinks, because he also believes he's a girl-magnet. You should have seen him flirting with poor Laurel. If she had been the one to inherit, he'd have dumped Gwen and married Laurel. But she got only a small trust fund. The guy hits on every girl he sees."

"Is that a warning?" Nancy gave him a flirtatious smile.

"Knowing Lawrence, it's a prediction." Cris lowered his voice as they came close to the table. "But I'll warn you that Gwen is the jealous type. Fool around with Lawrence, and you might have another chimney fall on you."

Nancy was already thinking about that convenient collapse as she sat down at the dinner table. From the comments she'd heard from her hiding place, she knew that Lawrence had noticed her. Would Gwen push down a chimney on a possible rival? Cris's words about Laurel and Lawrence came back to her. Might Gwen have stabbed an earlier rival?

Shaking her head, Nancy pushed those ideas aside. No way could Gwen have been on the lawn, ringing the dinner bell, and up on the roof, pushing the chimney down.

Lawrence, however, was still missing. He came hurrying out the french doors as Gwen served plates of cold crab salad. "So sorry," he said. "I was upstairs washing up when the bell rang."

Or were you upstairs washing brick dust off yourself *after* the bell rang? Nancy wondered.

"Well, you're here now," Gwen said. "Let's eat."

What followed was one of the most difficult meals Nancy had ever sat through. Gwen didn't speak to Buff or Nancy, but Lawrence was talking and smiling at Nancy—or rather, at Mandy Dean.

Cris tried to fill the silence by telling about the collapsing chimney.

"I heard the noise," Gwen said. "But I figured no one would be over there, so we could examine the damage after dinner."

She didn't seem brokenhearted to learn that "Mandy" had almost gotten buried in toppling bricks, Nancy thought.

Cris tried to talk about renovating the mansion, but there was nothing to discuss. While his brother and sister agreed with him, they weren't making any money to help pay for repairs. No one mentioned Stafford Bellamy's will or the court case that was holding up the inheritances. Nancy figured it was better to have silence than screaming.

She made an attempt to pinpoint Lawrence's whereabouts at the time the chimney fell. "Did you see it come down?" she asked, giving him a wide-eyed look.

"I barely heard it," Lawrence said with a shrug. "Must have been on the other side of this mausoleum." He gave her a smiling once-over. "But it would have been a shame if the chimney had actually landed on you. Where'd you meet this lovely creature, Buff?"

"Florida," Buff replied quickly, wrapping a possessive arm around Nancy's shoulders. "I was down there, racing in the winter season—"

He went into several long, boring stories about racing, occasionally turning to Nancy to say, "Remember?" or "Right, babe?"

Maybe he thinks he's protecting me from the big, bad wolf, Nancy thought sourly. But what he's managing to do is keep me from questioning Lawrence.

Nancy's eyes were glazing over when Gwen finally cut into the flood of reminiscences, her voice nasty. "Maybe Laurel enjoyed your racing stories, but I don't think Mandy is interested." She bobbed her head briefly at Nancy. "And I know no one else wants to hear them."

In the embarrassed silence that followed, Buff's arm slipped off Nancy's shoulders. His face went blank, and he seemed to zone out, raising his fork to his mouth and chewing almost mechanically.

This is a great bunch I've gotten myself involved with, Nancy thought.

When the meal finally ended, she turned to Cris Bellamy. "Maybe you, your sister, and your brother should take a look at that chimney now. See what the damage is." She managed to give a convincing shudder. "Me, I don't want to see."

Cris rose. So did Gwen and Buff.

"Coming, Lawrence?" Gwen asked, glancing back at her fiancé.

"I think I'll stay and keep Mandy company," Lawrence replied.

Gwen must have forgotten about their plan for

Lawrence to question "Mandy." If looks could kill, both Lawrence and Nancy would have been struck dead on the patio. Nancy couldn't see Lawrence's face as he turned to Gwen. But with a flip of her light brown hair, the heiress shrugged and spun on her heel.

Nancy and Lawrence were the only two left at the table. "You sure know what buttons to push with your fiancée," Nancy said.

"Gwen wants me to get the story on you," Lawrence said, smiling. "I figure now is as good a time as any to find out."

"I didn't think a tricky lawyer would be so up-front with his questions," Nancy said teasingly.

"I didn't think I'd have to trick anything out of you," Lawrence shot back, still smiling. "So what's the story, Mandy Dean?"

"Not much of a story. I come from a town not far from Chicago. Last year I went down to Florida for spring break—it beat the snow—and met Buff. I cheered for him at the races, and we got to be . . . friends."

"Good friends?" Lawrence pressed.

"Good enough to know when he needs a helping hand," Nancy replied, moving around so the table was between them. "I'm here on a job interview, and I saw Buff's face all over the newspapers. He looked as though he could use a friend."

Resting her hands on the table, Nancy leaned

forward and shot off a question of her own. "So what's the story on you, lawyer-man?"

"You really want to know, Mandy?" Lawrence's smile turned bitter. "I've got a fine old name without the money to go with it. My father lost all his money and worked himself to death trying to get it back. Philadelphia is a town that has dynasties of lawyers. But my father's firm is down to one old fossil who works out of his house to do an occasional will."

Lawrence leaned across the table himself. "I work for one of the big firms that drove my father out of business. I got hired only because of my name. They trot me out to make nice with society types who do business with the firm."

"Sounds like a great job," Nancy said. "No wonder you want to marry a rich girl."

He raised a protesting hand. "Hey, don't get me wrong. I really care about Gwen."

Nancy decided to press hard. "Then why were you flirting with me over dinner? I heard you even flirted with that dead girl—Laurel."

Lawrence looked hard at her for a moment, his eyebrows rising. "Now, who would have told you that? Not Buff. It would have to be Cris."

"Is it true?"

Lawrence's sharp but handsome features shifted. "Laurel was like a ray of sunshine in that gloomy family. The others, whether they admitted it or not, were just waiting for the old man to die. Cris wanted to take over the company. Gwen wanted to take her proper place in society. And Buff was only happy going *vroom-vroom* in his expensive toys."

Lawrence looked away, his face losing its hard edge for a moment. "Laurel was like a daughter to the old guy, but she didn't expect anything from him. She was studying to be a teacher—something useful, she always said." He glanced back at Nancy. "You know, I should have hated her. Laurel's father was the one who wiped out my dad."

His expression became sharp again. "You know, Mandy Dean, you got me to spill a lot more about myself and the Bellamys than you told me about yourself. I think maybe you've got a much more cunning mind than you let on."

Nancy was glad to see Buff and the others returning from their inspection. "We think we can get by with minor repairs," Cris said. "Nothing else looks ready to fall down."

Nancy walked over to Buff and took him by the arm. "Maybe now we can have that guided tour you promised," she said.

Buff took Nancy around the outside of the house, talking about architecture and other places where the mansion might be falling down. Nancy noticed that in some places the climbing ivy was so thick that it would be possible for a person to climb it to the roof—especially from the second floor windows.

"And, of course, here's Fort Bellamy," he said, leading Nancy to the ramshackle stables. The place smelled of old hay and looked abandoned, but the old tack room had been redone in wood paneling. As Buff flicked on a switch, Nancy gasped.

Indirect lighting gleamed off rank after rank of toy soldiers arrayed on wooden shelves. Nancy saw everything from armored Greek warriors with long spears to modern machine gunners, perfectly scaled to one inch high. There had to be thousands of figurines in the collection.

In the center of the room was a construction that looked like a pool table turned into a sandbox. Hills and plains had been sculpted out of the sand. Houses, villages, and forests composed of tiny trees were scattered around. Massed on this miniature terrain were still more toy soldiers. A huge army in blue uniforms led by the tricolor flag of France attacked a thin red line of British troops under the Union Jack.

"Uncle Stafford was fascinated by military history," Buff explained. "He'd use this sand table to duplicate the countryside of famous battlefields and refight the battles with his collection of soldiers."

He smiled in memory. "When we visited as kids, Cris and I would sometimes be allowed to be assistants, moving the troops around. But the orders always came from Uncle Stafford. He claimed that matching wits with the old generals—especially Napoleon—kept him on his toes for running his business."

Buff's smile faded. "I guess this was the battle my uncle was working on when he died."

"I can't believe your uncle turned the stables into a private war game palace!" Nancy exclaimed.

"Well, less messy than keeping the horses around," Buff replied. "There's a horse farm nearby, and my uncle boarded our couple of mounts there."

"Sounds great," Nancy said. "What do you say we go for a ride?" She and Buff had things to talk about, and here was a chance to get away from the mansion.

As Nancy went upstairs to change into a pair of jeans, she heard Buff explaining their planned outing.

After a brief drive in Nancy's car, they reached the horse farm. The stablemaster knew Buff and spent quite a while asking about his racing career.

Buff looked a little embarrassed as they finally mounted. "Old Mr. Frazier has known me since I was a kid. He's also a sports nut."

"And a bit of a fan, I think," Nancy said, smiling. "Whoa!" She reined in the dappled mare she was riding. The horse was a little too excited over getting out of its stall for an evening ride.

"That's behind me now," Buff said. "No more racing."

"How do you feel about horse racing?" Nancy asked, grinning. She let her frisky mount break into a canter, heading across a grassy field. Buff followed. It wasn't exactly a race. Like the horses, they were just burning off excess energy.

Buff caught up and led the way off the farm. They slowed to a walk as he guided his horse through a break in the wall of hedges by the roadside.

"We used to call this the secret entrance to the estate," he told Nancy as her horse followed. It leads to a bridle path—"

His words were interrupted as a plump man in a safari suit leaped out of the bushes. Nancy didn't need to look at his acne-scarred face to recognize him. The heavy camera in his hands was reminder enough.

"Hey, honey, Buff—smile!" The paparazzo snapped shot after shot, the strobe flashing.

It was too much for Nancy's nervous horse. With a squeal of fear, the mare reared, and Nancy found herself flying into the air.

Chapter Eleven

NANCY CLAMPED HER KNEES to the frantic horse's body and her arms around the animal's neck. She landed in the saddle but was nearly thrown off by the jolt as the mare's forefeet hit the ground again.

The pressure of Nancy's legs achieved two things: it kept her on the horse, and it also cut down on her mount's breathing. But the mare reared again before Nancy could regain control.

In that brief amount of time, the paparazzo had finished shooting pictures and dashed onto the road. A car rolled up, and he jumped in. Nancy could hear the photographer's laughter over the sound of squealing tires.

Nancy got off her horse and patted the trembling animal to calm it. Buff slid from his saddle. The fun had gone out of their ride.

"I've had it," Buff said angrily. "Let's go back." Together, they began to lead their mounts back to the stables.

"That—that—" Buff bit back whatever names he'd been about to call the photographer as another thought hit him. "How did he know we were here?"

The same question had been troubling Nancy. They were nowhere near the gates of the Orbeck estate, where photographers might lie in wait. If the paparazzo had been there, wouldn't he have shot them in Nancy's car, coming out? How could he have known about the bridle paths and the gap in the hedge?

Their answer came as they pushed through the shrubbery—and found Lawrence Harleigh.

"You!" Nancy gasped.

Lawrence gave her a mocking smile. "Ah. Clever but naive. Didn't expect that, did you?"

"How—" Buff began.

"Why—" Nancy said in the same breath.

"The 'how' part is easy," Lawrence said. "I've had photographers pestering me to set up photo opportunities since this whole circus started. One of the more persistent ones traced you here to Orbeck. He gave me his number, so I called him after I heard where you were headed."

Lawrence turned to Nancy. "As for 'why . . .'

Well, I thought you should find out what it's like to live in the Bellamy fishbowl as soon as possible. If there's anything in your life you'd like to keep hidden, get out now. Call it a start to your education."

"And what would you call *this?*" Buff unleashed a furious punch that laid Lawrence flat on his back. He was hauling his sister's fiancé to his feet again for another swing when Nancy grabbed his arm.

"Buff! Don't! He's not worth it!" She could feel the muscles of Buff's arm quivering under her fingers.

For a long moment, Buff held Lawrence at arm's length. Then he made a disgusted noise and tossed Harleigh to the ground.

Nancy didn't even stop to make sure Lawrence was all right. She just grabbed the reins on the horses and led them after Buff.

As Nancy strode along, she frowned in thought. Once again the guy she was trying to prove innocent of murder had displayed a killer's temper.

Still worse, that photographer had caught her with Buff—and gotten a picture of her face. Her cover was in serious danger of being blown.

The next morning Joe Hardy had a big smile on his face as he walked through the breakfast crowd in the dining room of the Stratford Hotel.

"Here's the paper you asked me to get," he said, handing a newspaper to Frank, who was already seated at a table.

"But look at what I got!" he cackled, holding up the other paper he'd picked up at the hotel's newsstand. Actually, calling *Truth Weekly* a newspaper was stretching the point, he thought. It was a tabloid, the sort of paper people picked up at supermarkets to get the hottest news on Bigfoot and UFOs. Sometimes, however, there would be a regular news story so sensational that *Truth Weekly* would get into the act.

"This time, they've outdone themselves," Joe said with a chuckle as he showed the front page to his brother. The headline, in huge letters, read, "Horsing Around?"

Under it was a full-page picture showing a startled-looking Buff Bellamy on a horse. Behind him, Nancy Drew seemed on the point of being thrown from the horse she was riding.

"Let me see that." Frank Hardy dropped the paper he was reading and snatched Joe's.

"Come on," Joe said as he let his brother read. "Who cares if your girlfriend gets a little egg on her face?"

But Frank sank back in relief as he scanned the photo caption. "It just calls her Buff's 'beautiful companion.'" He glared at Joe. "And she's *not* my girlfriend!"

"Then why are you so worried about her?"

"Knowing Nancy, she's down in Orbeck, investigating Buff's family undercover." Frank angrily tapped the newspaper. "If this rag identified her as Nancy Drew, her cover would be blown, and she could be in danger."

Joe stubbornly shook his head. "The murderer knows who she is because she's the one trying to get him off."

"We've got to get a warning to her about where this picture ended up," Frank said, ignoring Joe's remark. "But first"—he grinned at Joe—"I've got an idea how to plug those press leaks that have been screwing up the investigation."

"What's that?" Joe asked.

"The Vidocq people are going after Bellamy Holdings' accounting system, trying to find something fishy. But if they're looking for OC involvement, there may be an easier way to link the leaks."

"I hear you talking, but the words don't make any sense," Joe complained.

"You'll understand. After breakfast we're going to the scene of the crime," Frank said cryptically.

"What's this 'scene of the crime' stuff?"

"You'll see," Frank said as the waiter arrived to take their orders.

After breakfast Frank led the way out of the hotel and down Broad Street.

"Are you going to tell me where we're going?" Joe asked, striding along beside Frank.

"Nope," Frank said, enjoying stringing his brother along.

Frank guided them to the building where the Vidocq Society held its meetings.

"What do you think you're going to find here?" Joe's tone of voice suggested he didn't want to know.

"This is where the first leak occurred," Frank pointed out. "It happened in a room full of law-enforcement types—and several waiters and a bartender. Resnick mentioned that there were organized-crime problems in one of the local restaurant unions. So we look for people on the staff with possible OC ties—or grudges against the police."

"You're just looking for trouble." Frank could see that Joe was not happy. "And I think you'll make a fool of yourself with this crackpot theory. There are a lot more suspects than just the waiters. The leaks could have started from a Vidocq member. All anyone had to do was mention the investigation to a wife or a husband or somebody at work. There are enough cops who didn't like how Buff got away with murder. Why don't you think about them?"

Frank laughed. "If I thought about them, *you'd* be the number-one leak suspect."

Joe shut up as the elevator reached the floor with the luncheon club.

The club manager remembered the Hardys as Will Resnick's special guests. He was outraged at the suggestion that the press leaks could have originated from his staff, but he agreed to help.

"Most of our people have been with us for years," the manager said. "None of them have had any trouble with the law."

"Nobody got nervous or annoyed when the club served all those police people?" Frank pressed.

The manager frowned, thinking for a moment. "I wouldn't exactly say anyone got nervous. But Martin, one of the bartenders—he said something odd when he heard about the Vidocq Society and its membership." The frown deepened as the man tried to remember. "It was something like, that was just what he needed."

"Tell me about this Martin," Frank said.

"Martin Smith—he's our replacement man, working if one of the regular bartenders can't come in. He's been with us only a few weeks. I don't think anybody knows him that well."

"Was he working for the last Vidocq luncheon," Frank asked.

The manager nodded. "One of our regular bartenders was sick, and Martin was filling in. As a matter of fact, he's still filling in today."

Frank thanked the man. Then the Hardys headed for the bar. It was empty at that time of day, but the bartender was already there, setting things up for the noontime rush.

"Martin Smith?" Frank asked the man, who he guessed was in his early thirties.

The bartender looked up. His long, lank hair hung around his face. "Who wants to know?"

Frank shot a glance at his brother. That wasn't the answer of an innocent man. "We're just a couple of people who enjoyed lunch here a few days ago. Remember the big group? The Vidocq Society? All those cops?"

The bartender picked up a glass and began to polish it, but his hands were trembling. "I remember," he said. "What happened? Somebody lose his badge?"

"No, it's a case of loose lips," Frank replied. "Somebody blabbed to the press about what was being discussed in this room." He gave Smith a hard stare. "*You* were in this room, weren't you?"

"Not that it's a crime," Joe put in. "We just want to find out who's talking and ask them to stop."

Frank glared at his brother. It sounded like Joe was trying to be a nice guy, the "good cop" to Frank's scary "bad cop." The only problem was that Joe was being *too* nice. They'd never be able to scare information out of Smith if this kept up.

"No, talking isn't a crime," Frank said, swinging back to Martin Smith. "But I've got to wonder why someone would do it. The easiest reason would be that they hate cops. And what kind of person would that be? Maybe a person who'd been *caught* by the cops, who had a police record—"

That pushed the right button. Smith went pale. Then with unexpected agility he vaulted over the bar and ran out of the dining room.

Frank whipped around in quick pursuit. After a second, Joe got over his surprise and dashed after his brother.

Smith sprinted down the main hall of the club. Since it was well before noon, there were few club members or staff to block the way.

The only people in the hall had already jumped aside as the Hardys came roaring through. Ahead of them, Smith flung himself into a left turn.

That's where the elevators are, Frank thought, but we'll be on him before one arrives.

Smith didn't stop at the elevators, however. He darted past them up a dead-end corridor.

No, Frank realized, it wasn't a dead end. There was a fire door tucked into an inconspicuous corner. Smith smashed into the door, which flew open.

Frank heard a high, tweeting noise as he bombed through the doorway. The exit must have been wired, he thought. That's the alarm.

Below him, Martin Smith was leaping down the stairs two at a time, trying for the best speed possible. It wasn't easy. This stairway was old-fashioned, nearly a death trap for people trying to escape a fire. The stairs were steep, the treads narrow, and there were twenty flights before they reached ground level. Racing down them was more like skiing than running. But skiers didn't have to swoop through a 180-degree spin on every landing.

Frank's heel skidded off a step. A frantic grab at the handrail saved him from a disastrous fall.

Smith wasn't as lucky. He slipped, too, and his stumble turned into a plunge. With cries of pain, he fell and bounced down half a flight of stairs before landing on his back on the landing below.

"Gotcha now!" Frank rasped as he charged down.

But Smith was rolling to his feet. He had something in his hand—a derringer, a tiny two-shot gun. The weapon looked like a toy, but Frank knew that it could kill.

And the desperate man had it pointed straight at Frank's head.

Chapter Twelve

"STAY BACK!" Martin Smith hissed at Frank.

Joe Hardy gasped in horror as he saw the bartender aim the miniature gun. Frank was too far away even to make a grab for it. He'd need at least two steps to get in range. By that time he'd have two holes in his head.

As for Joe, he was even farther away, almost at the top of the flight of stairs. He knew he'd never make it down in time to help.

Not if he ran.

There was another way, though. Joe flexed his legs and flung himself into the air.

Smith's eyes grew wide at the sight of Joe apparently flying down at him. As he stared the derringer wobbled slightly in his hand, veering off-target. Frank rushed forward, going low.

Joe was already coming in from on high. He landed on them both, knocking Smith down into the stairwell. But even as they were falling, Joe used a fist to club the gun from the bartender's grasp. The little weapon skittered across the gray-painted concrete landing.

It took an effort for Joe to stand up, especially since he was hauling Smith to his feet, too. Keeping his hold on the two handfuls of shirt front, Joe shook the bartender. "What was the idea of pulling a stupid stunt like that?" he demanded.

"I think that pulling a gun on me rates as more than a stupid stunt," Frank Hardy declared in fury.

"Wasn't going to shoot," a still-breathless Martin Smith insisted. "Just trying to get you to—to back off."

"You ran for it when my brother mentioned prison records," Joe said.

Smith nodded. "I've got one," he admitted. "Right now I'm out on parole—and I haven't been able to get a job. My brother-in-law set up this bartending gig. He's some kind of big wheel in the union—"

A light dawned in Joe's head. "And I bet he's connected to some mob or other. But guys on parole aren't supposed to be in contact with known felons."

Smith nodded. "They could send me back to prison for that." His eyes burned with fear. "I'm not going back there! You don't know what it's like! I'd rather blow myself away first!"

"Is that why you were carrying this peashooter?" Frank inquired, picking up the little derringer. "Guys on parole aren't supposed to carry guns. Or are things different in Pennsylvania?"

"I live in a rathole in a dangerous neighborhood, so I carry a little protection." Smith sounded defiant, but Frank noted that the man's shoulders were slumped in defeat.

"We could put you back in prison for the rest of your sentence," Joe said slowly. "Plus maybe an extra few years for playing with guns and aiming them at people."

Smith shrank into himself.

"Or," Joe went on, "maybe we can do you a favor—if you do us one."

Smith perked up a little, while Frank looked confused.

"You have to give us the straight story," Joe warned. "Did you leak anything you heard at the Vidocq meeting to the press?"

Smith was taken completely by surprise. "No," he said. "Why should I?"

"Have you heard anything among the other waiters or bartenders—maybe among mob-connected guys—about giving the cops' club any trouble in its latest investigation?"

"No," Smith said. "I didn't hear anything about that."

"Think carefully," Joe warned. "I'm giving you a chance. Don't blow it."

"I'd have heard if something like that was going down," Smith insisted. "My brother-in-law would have told me."

Joe glanced at Frank, then turned to Smith again. "Here's my offer. We take that gun and turn it over to one of our cop friends, with some sort of story about how we found it. You go back upstairs to work, keep your head down and your mouth shut. Have we got a deal?"

Frank was nearly ready to blow up. "This guy almost blows me away. And your idea of punishment is to take his gun away and give him a lecture?"

Joe stuck his face in Frank's and matched him glare for glare. "What do you want?" he asked. "You can waste time working on a police report for an assault you made happen—by pushing a scared man. Or you can work on a real case. Which is it going to be?"

Frank opened his mouth, then closed it with an audible snap.

"I take that as an agreement to letting Smith go," Joe said.

"Go." Frank's voice came out between clenched teeth.

"I think we'll have to go up, too," Joe said, heading through the fire doors for the elevators. "We've got a chase and a false fire alarm to explain away."

Joe talked fast when they returned to the dining club. The manager wasn't happy, but they managed to call off the fire department and keep the building from being evacuated. Joe made no mention of a gun and pleaded that their "misunderstanding" shouldn't be held against Martin Smith.

At last the Hardys boarded the elevator for the ground floor. "One theory down," Joe said in satisfaction.

"You'll have to eliminate a lot more people before I'll buy your favorite candidate," Frank said, still angry.

"Come on!" Joe complained. "Buff has—"

"We know what Buff has. You've talked about it often enough," Frank cut him off. "But we've also got Nancy checking into just why Gwen Bellamy is so angry. And why Cris Bellamy was so evasive when we tried to talk to him."

Joe sighed.

But Frank was on a roll. "We may also want to ask Gwen's fiancé how he feels about the money his family lost in the failure of Bellamy and Kendall. For that matter, there are the Bellamys themselves. Did they know that Laurel's dad wiped them out? Of course, we have the too-nervous Richard Tacey. And there might be someone we don't even know about yet with a grudge against both the Bellamys *and* the Kenways. . . ."

"Stop!" Joe begged. "At this rate, we're going

to have the whole population of Philadelphia on our suspect list."

The elevator reached the ground floor, and the doors opened. As the Hardys walked back to their hotel, neither of them was in a good mood.

They came in through the main entrance of the Stratford Hotel and set off across the lobby for the elevators. Just then a figure rose from one of the lobby couches. At first Joe couldn't even tell if it was male or female. He merely saw a shapeless navy raincoat, a floppy tweed hat, and sunglasses.

Then he caught a glimpse of reddish blond hair and heard the desperate voice. "Where have you guys been?"

Joe had to bite his lip to keep from bursting into laughter. The badly dressed stranger was Nancy Drew.

Frank tried to handle the situation with a little class. "Why don't we go upstairs and discuss things?"

In the boys' room, Nancy gladly got rid of her improvised disguise. "It was just stuff I could borrow from around the house out there. I didn't mind looking ridiculous—as long as I didn't look recognizable."

"Oh, I just thought it was one of your clever undercover disguises," Joe joked.

Nancy ignored Joe's remark. Frank could see she was distracted—and worried. "Have you seen the cover of—"

"Of today's *Truth Weekly*?" Frank finished for her.

"Wouldn't have missed it for the world," Joe said, still grinning. "Do you need some extras for your scrapbook? We've got one."

He held up the copy he'd bought downstairs, pretending to examine the cover. "Maybe not the most flattering picture but nice enough. You look just like a cowgirl, up on that horse. Maybe this newfound fame can turn into big bucks for you. Some Hollywood producer might spot this photo—and they're making a lot of cowgirl movies these days."

Enjoying his little act, Joe pointed to the horse. "This shows you can ride." Then he pointed to Nancy's face in the photo. "And look how expressive your face is! I see anger and surprise, not to mention embarrassment. . . ."

Frank braced himself, expecting a thermonuclear explosion from Nancy. But none came. In fact she seemed to be shrinking in on herself.

Something must be *very* wrong, Frank thought.

But Joe wouldn't give up. Reaching for a hotel pen, he asked, "So, do you think you could autograph this for us?"

"Joe, why don't you just shut up?" Frank finally burst out. "You're not being funny. The only thing that's keeping Nancy from wiping the floor with you is the fact that she obviously has other problems, *bigger* problems than your sniping."

Joe stood openmouthed for a moment, staring at his brother. Then he turned to Nancy. "Yeah. You don't look like your usual self. And I'm not talking about the interesting wardrobe you showed up in."

"What's the problem, Nancy?" Frank asked. "Can we help? Is it something to do with the case?"

"You might say it has something to do with the case." Nancy's shoulders slumped. "It has everything to do with that stupid picture. I don't know if Mr. Resnick told you, but I've gone undercover in Philadelphia high society."

She sighed. "Unfortunately, there's another socialite in town—one you both know."

Joe frowned in puzzlement. "Who?"

"Brenda Carlton," Nancy said in a dull voice.

As soon as he heard the name, Frank grimaced. Brenda Carlton was a young reporter from Nancy's hometown of River Heights.

Actually, "reporter" sort of stretched the truth. Her father owned a local newspaper, and Brenda sometimes wrote articles. She thought of herself as an investigative journalist, a rival to Nancy. From what Frank had seen, however, Brenda came off more as a Nancy Drew wannabe.

Still, lack of ability hadn't stopped her from nearly ruining several of Nancy's cases in the past, and that included a case the Hardys had also worked on in River Heights.

"Brenda is in town?" Frank said each word slowly.

"Yes. And she's seen today's *Truth Weekly,* too."

"Uh-oh," Joe said, seeing where the conversation was going.

"She called up the Orbeck estate this morning—right after she saw the paper," Nancy said. "It was just lucky that Buff answered the phone because she'd have blown my cover otherwise."

"That's what she's threatening to do anyway, isn't it?" Frank asked quietly.

Nancy nodded. "She wants me to have a little chat with her—tell her all about our investigation."

"Or?" Joe asked.

Dejected, Nancy looked down at the floor. "Or the whole world finds out the name of Buff's companion in that picture."

Chapter Thirteen

"WHEN AND WHERE are you supposed to meet Brenda?" Joe Hardy asked.

Nancy glanced at her watch. "In about fifteen minutes. That's why I'm glad to see you guys. As for the place, well, at least it's nearby." Nancy managed the ghost of a smile. "Brenda wants to meet at the Liberty Bell."

"Oh, nice," Frank said disgustedly. "Mix in a little sightseeing with her blackmail."

"Want us to come with you?" Joe offered.

"Thanks." Nancy smiled. "Boy, I must *really* look sad for you to offer your help."

"It was the hat," Frank gently joked. "Joe hates to admit it, but he's just a sucker for girls in floppy hats."

Nancy had enough time to stop by her hotel to

don a better raincoat and a scarf to hide her hair. She and the Hardys left through a side exit. A seven-block walk brought them to Independence Hall Historical Park.

"We should come in from the Market Street side. Brenda will be at the entrance to the pavilion where they keep the Liberty Bell," Nancy said. She walked up to the glass doors of the modernistic little building, slipping off her sunglasses but keeping the scarf over her hair.

Afternoon sunlight poured through a long skylight in the roof of the pavilion. It glowed off the wooden panels in the hallway that led to the exhibit hall. The Liberty Bell itself stood silhouetted against a huge glass wall that looked out across the park to Independence Hall in the distance.

A Park Service guard was giving a lecture to a group of tourists, but one person in the back of the crowd wasn't listening. Nancy glanced over. Yes, it was Brenda Carlton.

Very red lipstick made Brenda's smile gleam as she turned to see her rival coming down the hallway. Brenda was a pretty girl, with long, dark hair. Seeing her now, Nancy thought that the girl reporter's features looked a little on the sharp side.

Huh, she thought. Brenda and Lawrence Harleigh would make a perfect couple. Certainly, they'd be considered soulmates. Both seemed to be working overtime at blowing Nancy's investigation out of the water.

"Why, Nancy—or should I say, *Mandy,*" Brenda almost purred. Her smile slipped for a moment when she saw the Hardys appear behind Nancy. But Brenda had the upper hand. Nancy knew there was nothing Frank or Joe could do to stop her.

Brenda obviously felt the same way. "And you brought your friends. Nice to see you again."

The lecture ended, and tourists began taking photos. Catching Nancy and Frank by the arm, Brenda left the pavilion. Joe followed as Brenda set off across the park. "We'll go for a stroll," she said. "Too crowded in here. And I'm sure, with all you've got to tell me, that you'd prefer it stayed private."

"What are you doing here in Philadelphia?" Frank demanded.

"Just down here on a story," Brenda said airily. "I got a tip two days ago—anonymous phone call, whispered voice, the works. The tipster said Nancy was here, trying to prove that hunky Buff Bellamy was innocent."

Brenda smiled. "To tell the truth, I thought the calls were some nut's idea of a joke. Then came the wire service stories about you and the Vidocq Society looking into the murder. I got Dad to let me check it out. And when I got here this morning, *who* do I find on the cover of *Truth Weekly* but my good friend Nancy Drew!"

Nancy felt like a mouse caught by a cat that liked to play with its food. But Frank had stopped in his tracks, causing the arm-locked threesome to spin around almost in half a circle.

"What is it?" Brenda demanded.

"The phantom leaker strikes again," Frank said, furious.

"What! Tell me!" Brenda implored.

"We've been tripped up every step of the way on this case by somebody giving information away—to the press and also to suspects. These leaks have already cost us some evidence and nearly got Joe and me killed."

Brenda quickly pulled a microcassette recorder out of her shoulder bag. "Say that again."

Frank paid no attention. He was looking over at Nancy. "I thought I had a theory on who was breaching our security, but it didn't pan out."

He looked at the girl reporter. "And what Brenda just said proves it. I believed we were being ratted out by people who didn't know us very well. But that's not so. Whoever called Brenda would have to know about her history with Nancy. More important, they'd have to know that Brenda exists."

"People know me," Brenda said in hurt tones. "I've written stories . . ."

"Sure—stories that were printed in River Heights," Frank cut in. "But has any of your stuff made the national press services? Would anything with your name on it have been printed, say, in Philadelphia?"

"Um—" Brenda looked down. "Probably not." Then her head popped up again. "But this story could do that for me."

She glared at Nancy. "You owe me, believe it or not. I talked to my dad this morning, and he's already seen that *Truth Weekly* cover. He could go with a front page story identifying you, but I told him this was *my* story and to hold off—that I could get a bigger scoop. So," she said smugly, "I got him to hold off . . . so far. But I need a good story—an exclusive—and quick."

Nancy looked at Frank and Joe, then shrugged in defeat. "All right," she said through gritted teeth. "I *am* trying to prove that Buff Bellamy is innocent in the killing of Laurel Kenway. My dad and I approached a group here in Philadelphia—"

"The Vidocq Society," Brenda interrupted. "I read about them."

"And I guess you know my father defended Buff in court, getting certain evidence dismissed—"

"Evidence that you guys found," Brenda said, turning her recorder toward the Hardys. "How did you feel about that?"

"Wait a minute," Frank said. "This is Nancy's interview."

"Well, if you refuse to help out . . ." There was an unspoken threat behind her words.

Nancy looked pleadingly at the boys.

Frank took a deep breath and let it out in a big sigh. "Yes, we did find the murder weapon. But it could have been planted in Buff's car. So we've been looking at other people who might have had a motive—"

"I'd be more interested to hear about how you nearly got killed," Brenda interrupted.

Nancy listened as Joe recounted the story of their visit to the penthouse private dining club and the sabotage of the elevator. "One thing is certain," he finished. "It was no accident."

"I wish I could be so sure about what happened to me yesterday," Nancy said. "A chimney nearly fell on my head. The problem is, the brickwork is so old and rotten that it could have fallen by itself."

"Or it could have been pushed," Frank finished grimly. "If that's the case, somebody might already have doubts about your cover."

"What *is* your cover?" Brenda chimed in. "I mean, you couldn't just stroll into that mansion."

"That's just what I did," Nancy said. "With a little help from Buff."

"What did he do?" Joe asked.

Nancy could feel her face getting warm.

"Nothing much. He just said I was a—ah—friend of his."

"Ooh," Brenda said, thrusting her recorder out farther. "And is Buff as much of a hunk in person as he seems in his pictures?"

"I thought this was supposed to be about the case," Frank complained.

"Well, Buff *is* the defendant in this whole thing. I'm trying to get a little human interest."

"Buff is a very nice guy who is innocent," Nancy said. "He's trying to get his life back together, but he'll never be able to do that until we prove he didn't kill Laurel Kenway."

"Just out of curiosity," Joe asked, "where was Buff when that chimney fell?"

"He was at the dinner table with his sister, Gwen. His brother, Cris, helped get me out of the crash zone. But Gwen's slimy fiancé, Lawrence Harleigh, was late getting to supper. He said he'd been upstairs washing his hands when the bricks came tumbling down."

"So when did this Harleigh guy become slimy?" Frank asked.

"He hit on me after dinner, then set me up for that photographer to snap my picture." Nancy grimaced. "I'm told he used to flirt with Laurel Kenway."

"Great," Joe muttered. "Add one more to the army of suspects in this case."

"We don't think there's an organized crime

connection after all," Frank said, taking a moment to explain the theory Will Resnick had suggested. "But there *is* an old business scandal that involved Laurel's father, Walter Kenway. He was Stafford Bellamy's partner and wound up in jail for fraud. He wiped out a bunch of investors."

"And now we have a dead Bellamy—Stafford—and a dead Kenway—Laurel." Nancy frowned as her thoughts raced.

"The list of people who took a bath when the company crashed reads like the Philadelphia society register," Frank went on.

"But you'll love the high points," Joe said. "Among those who lost their fortunes are the parents of Gwen, Cris, and Buff—"

"And Lawrence Harleigh's father," Nancy finished. She smiled at Joe's disappointment. "He mentioned something about it while he was flirting with me."

"You must like to live dangerously," Joe said. "Gwen Bellamy intends to marry that guy, and she's got quite a temper."

"Tell me about it," Nancy said. "I overheard her wishing I was dead."

"Was that before or after the chimney fell on you?" Frank asked.

"Before," Nancy said. "But I don't think she really meant it."

"I wouldn't be so sure," Frank said.

"I thought about it. Gwen couldn't have pushed that chimney on me. She was downstairs, getting dinner."

"But this Lawrence Harleigh was upstairs. Did he hear her say she wished you were dead?"

"He was the one who started joking about killing me," Nancy said.

"Was that before or after he hit on you?" Joe asked with a grin.

"Hey, guys," Brenda spoke up, clicking off her recorder.

Nancy blushed. She'd almost forgotten Brenda's presence.

The reporter was annoyed. "This stuff is all nice enough—"

"And exclusive," Joe added.

"Yeah. A *boring* exclusive," Brenda complained.

"What about us nearly getting killed?" Joe protested.

"And me?" Nancy said.

Brenda shrugged. "Do you have the bad guy? No. All you've got is a lot of theories, and even more suspects.

"All in all, this is maybe a page three story. Identifying you as the girl in that *Truth Weekly*—that's front page. If I know my dad, that's what he'll go with."

Nancy's jaw dropped. "But we gave you everything you wanted."

"And a lot more," Brenda gleefully agreed. She arched an eyebrow and smiled maliciously. "Looks like you were so rattled over all this, you didn't think to ask for any promises in return—like spiking the picture story."

"But I—we assumed—" Nancy started to say. Her rival's smile grew broader.

Brenda widened her eyes and looked innocently at Nancy. "Did I promise anything?" She turned to the Hardys. "Did *you* hear me promise anything?"

"You lousy little blackmailer!" Frank Hardy burst out. "Then everything we said is off the record!"

"That's not on my tape," Brenda said, putting her recorder away. "And it will be my word against yours—uh-uh, don't do anything stupid," she said when Frank reached for her bag. Brenda nodded to her right, where a Federal park ranger was giving them a long look.

"If you want to do anything, thin out those suspects. Maybe you can still get me a hotter story."

"You've got to give us some time," Nancy begged.

"Maybe I can hold my dad off for another day." Brenda didn't look so sure now. "*Maybe.* This is hot news, and he doesn't want to get scooped. Look, I'm at the Barclay Hotel. If you've got anything more, you can call me there." With that, Brenda set off across the park.

Nancy looked after the other girl in disgust. Brenda's promise was obviously useless, she thought. They had to solve the case almost immediately—or her face could be on the front pages of papers across the country!

Chapter Fourteen

JOE WATCHED as Nancy made an attempt to smile. "Well, guys, things have to get better," she said.

Frank nodded glumly. "'Cause they can't get much worse."

"I hate to say 'I told you so,'" Joe said. "But I'd say we've gotten precisely nowhere with this investigation. Maybe, just maybe, Frank and I were right from the beginning." He shook his head. "I don't know what the Vidocq Society is going to do. But I think we'll be off the case after Brenda Carlton makes idiots of us all."

"Journalistic ethics is not her strong point," Nancy gloomily agreed. "Knowing her, she'll probably run *both* stories. We're going to be laughingstocks." She glanced around. "So if anybody has a rabbit to pull out of his hat, now is definitely the time to do it."

"I don't know if it's a rabbit," Frank said, "but there's something I'd like to try. We checked the finances of Bellamy Holdings with an FBI accountant and an IRS guy. The head man there, Richard Tacey, gave us their books for the last ten years. According to those records, the Bellamy company is more honest than some angels."

"So?" Nancy said.

"So why didn't our pal Mr. Tacey mention the big financial scandal at Bellamy and Kenway?"

Joe shrugged. "Maybe he wasn't with them back then."

"That wouldn't explain why he was sweating," Frank said. "I think he's got something to hide."

"Yeah?" Joe said sarcastically. "And we're such math whizzes that we can uncover it."

"I think we can get him off balance—if we triple-team him." Frank turned to Nancy with a gleam in his eye. "Look, I know you're mad at us. I also know we work well together. I've got a plan, but it needs you if it's going to work."

"That's one more plan than I've got," Nancy said. "Count me in."

"Good." Frank now turned to Joe. "Nancy and I have stuff to get ready. Why don't you head back to our hotel? We'll meet you there."

Joe stopped at a coffee shop for lunch, then returned to the room he shared with his brother.

He'd just found a good station on the radio and had his feet up on the bed when there was a knock at the door.

He jumped off the bed and went to answer it. "Can I help you?" he asked the woman outside. Then he gawked. "Nancy?"

Nancy had assumed a look very different from the way she usually dressed. She wore a dowdy, somewhat worn-looking blue suit that made her look heavier and older. Her hair was pulled back in a bun. And she had on an old-fashioned pair of eyeglasses that magnified her eyes slightly.

"Well," Joe admitted, "you certainly don't look like Buff Bellamy's 'beautiful companion.'"

"Thanks—I think," Nancy said, removing the glasses and rubbing the bridge of her nose. "We picked up the outfit in a local thrift shop, just in case you think I'd own such a thing. The glasses are some magnifying jobbies I got on sale in a shop downstairs in the hotel. I have to watch my step with them. But luckily we picked up these lovely flat-heeled shoes for me to wear."

The shoes looked as if they'd been designed for somebody with arthritis.

"Very attractive," Joe said. "And just who are you supposed to be?"

"I'll explain on the way to Tacey's office," Frank said as he came into the room.

For their second visit to Bellamy Holdings, Frank simply had them announced as returning

Vidocq investigators. This time, they weren't met in the outer reception area. They were ushered into Richard Tacey's private office.

"Ah—gentlemen . . . and, ah, ma'am." Tacey looked a little surprised to see the two teens with a strange woman.

"I'm afraid agents Portino and Sharpe couldn't make it," Frank said apologetically. "Agent Sharpe had a few more questions to ask. Since it got rather late yesterday, he sent Ms. Drew here to help us on the follow-up."

Tacey seemed more to be taking refuge behind his large desk than simply sitting at it. Since Rick Sharpe was the tax man, Joe knew that Tacey would then think Nancy was with the IRS.

The man was definitely beginning to sweat, Joe thought.

"Agent Sharpe told you to say these were just informal inquiries," Frank said.

That made Tacey sweat a little more, Joe saw.

"There surely couldn't be any irregularities in our financial records," Tacey said.

"No, these questions deal with a period from before the records you gave us," Frank said. "Were you involved with this company's predecessors—Bellamy and Kenway?"

"Ah, yes, I worked in a considerably more minor position," Tacey began.

As the executive spoke Nancy whipped a stenographer's pad and a pen from the big, battered plastic purse she carried. Quickly she began writing some strange symbols. Shorthand, Joe guessed.

"It was um—uh, years ago." Tacey's words stumbled to a stop, and so did Nancy's pen.

She brought her glasses down, glancing over them. Joe suspected she did it just so she could get a good look at Tacey. Wearing those magnifying lenses must have been giving her a headache. But the look she gave Tacey unconsciously imitated the killer glances Joe's third-grade teacher used to nail her more unruly students.

Tacey must have had a teacher like that, too, for he said somewhat nervously, "As I told you, I didn't have a very responsible post."

Nancy's pen dashed right along with his every word. "Don't worry," she said, bringing down her glasses. "I can keep up."

Even her voice sounded different—more nasal, Joe thought.

Frank nodded. "Was your minor position in the company the reason you didn't mention the fraud case back then?"

Beads of sweat gathered even more heavily on Tacey's forehead. "It *was* years ago."

"It must have been a blow for Mr. Bellamy to have his partner make off with so much of the company's money." Frank looked over at Tacey. "How lucky that he was able to save his half of the partnership—and your job."

"I—I don't understand," Tacey stammered.

"Well, I'm sure you remember that at his trial, Walter Kenway denied stealing any money. How did your company trace his thefts?"

"The investigation wasn't my responsibility." Tacey wasn't looking at Frank, but at Nancy's scribbling pen.

Joe was amazed. The executive was completely distracted.

"Weren't you surprised at how Stafford Bellamy took in the orphan daughter of the man who almost ruined him?"

"I'm an executive in Mr. Bellamy's company," Tacey said. "But I—I can't comment on his personal decisions." He glanced around—almost desperately, Frank thought. "If you want to hear about that, you should talk to Wallace Collingwood."

Joe stared. "Who?"

"I've heard that name before," Nancy said. "He was Stafford Bellamy's lawyer, I believe."

Tacey nodded. "He was also a close friend. Probably the only associate Mr. Bellamy really trusted."

Nancy frowned. "I understand Collingwood is in the hospital now."

"I—ah—believe so."

For some reason, Tacey looked even more nervous. As if he'd said the wrong thing.

"Thank you very much," Nancy said, closing

her notebook with a snap. "I'm sure Agent Sharpe will get back to you with any other questions."

They headed out the door and into the elevator.

"You were really impressive—especially with that shorthand," Joe complimented Nancy. "Even *I* was afraid of you."

Nancy laughed. "What shorthand?" she said. "I was just faking it."

The elevator reached the ground floor, and they headed for the lobby pay phones. Nancy dialed Orbeck and got Buff.

"Oh—Mandy," Joe heard him say. The younger Hardy craned his neck to listen in.

"I need to know about your uncle's lawyer, Wallace Collingwood."

"Uncle Collie?" Buff asked.

"What?"

"That's what we used to call him when we were kids. He was Uncle Stafford's closest friend."

"But he's in the hospital now, you said," Nancy pressed.

"Yeah—University Hospital. He's been in a pretty bad way, going back and forth from their nursing facility to intensive care. I suppose I should get down there and visit him—"

"Not today," Nancy said crisply. "We're going to try."

They arrived at the hospital in time for afternoon visiting hours. But the clerk at the information desk was not about to give them visitors' passes. "I'm afraid Mr. Collingwood is in intensive care. Only members of his family are allowed in."

"We're his nephews," Joe quickly replied.

"And his niece," Nancy added. "We were really hoping to see Uncle Collie. I came all the way from Chicago."

Perhaps it was the use of the pet nickname, but the woman relented. "Just fifteen minutes," she warned.

When they reached the intensive care unit, another nurse warned, "This hasn't been one of Mr. Collingwood's better days."

The rooms in the ward were arranged around a circular nursing station, like the sun's rays.

The three sleuths entered the room marked with Wallace Collingwood's name. Lying in a hospital bed was a painfully thin man. His eyes were closed, and his skin was beyond pale. It seemed almost transparent. Joe could make out a faint tracery of blood vessels on the side of Collingwood's head.

He was hooked up to a monitor, and there were IV tubes running into his arms. He lay frighteningly still.

"Maybe this is a bad idea," Joe muttered. He glanced around the room, feeling a little spooked. "The guy looks dead."

Frank glanced toward the big glass window

fronting the nursing station. "I think they would have noticed out there. Besides, the monitor would have gone off."

Nancy shot them both an upset look. "Don't say that. For all you know, Mr. Collingwood could hear you."

She walked over to the lawyer's still form, a sad expression on her face. "Maybe we should go," she whispered.

Joe gave a start of surprise as Nancy suddenly reached out. She placed a hand gently on Collingwood's forehead and let it rest there.

But Joe, Frank, and Nancy all jumped when the "dead man" opened his eyes to stare at them.

Chapter Fifteen

FRANK HARDY COULDN'T GET OVER what a difference a pair of eyes made. With his eyelids closed, Wallace Collingwood looked—well, dead.

But, eyes open, the elderly lawyer was very much alive. His eyes were a bright blue. As Collingwood moved his head to glance at Nancy, Joe, and Frank, it was like having a turret with heavy guns track around and aim at them.

No wonder this guy was a successful lawyer in his prime, Frank thought.

"Well, what do you three want?" Collingwood asked. Although his words came out in a whisper, the tone of his voice was demanding. "I know my relatives—they come dutifully by every once in a while to make sure I'm still alive. So at the very least, you're up here on false pretenses."

The difference between the glow of intelligence in Collingwood's eyes and the faintness of his voice was shocking. Frank realized they were dealing with a brilliant mind whose body had given out. He decided on the straightforward approach.

"Mr. Collingwood, this is Nancy Drew. I'm Frank Hardy, and this is my brother, Joe. We *are* here under false pretenses, but we have to ask some questions about Stafford Bellamy. He—ah, we—"

Frank suddenly realized they had a problem. Would anyone have told the very sick man that his best friend had died? It might be too much of a shock. How should they handle this?

Collingwood glared at him. "Don't get mealy-mouthed on me, son. I know that Stafford's dead. People have a bad habit when they think you're unconscious. They talk about things as if you can't hear."

The man's eyes took on a faraway look for a moment. "It's a terrible thing to lose a friend, especially when you don't have many left." His eyes shot to Frank again. "What do you want to know?"

Frank knew Collingwood was weak, so he got straight to the point. "We can't find anyone to tell us about the failure of Bellamy and Kenway. We asked Richard Tacey."

"A yes-man," Collingwood responded. "He's not a bad administrator, if you give him orders. Young Cris will have a time running the company—hmm. You want to know about Bellamy and Kenway, do you? A bad time for Stafford. For a while, he didn't know where he'd get the money to save his properties. I couldn't help—except to give legal advice when Kenway was arrested for fraud."

"Do you know why Mr. Bellamy took Laurel Kenway into his house?" Nancy asked. "It seems an odd thing to do if her father nearly ruined him."

Collingwood nodded. "It was one of the few truly generous things I ever saw Stafford do. He got nothing in return—except the company of a very bright, cheerful young woman. Took his brother Bart's children in, too. But they stood to inherit. Good kids, but the expectation of getting rich when someone dies—it does things to people. I've had it myself, with relatives coming by like vultures. People walking on eggshells, afraid of getting cut out of the will."

He shook his head. "Laurel wasn't like that at all. She enjoyed Stafford's estate and such. But as soon as she was old enough, she planned out her own life. Laurel was studying to be a teacher. She got into the university on her own efforts, with a scholarship. Of all the people around Stafford, she was the least impressed about any sort of inheritance." The old lawyer frowned. "I wonder how that turned out."

"Well, you ought to know," Joe said. "You wrote up the will."

Collingwood's sharp eyes focused on him. "So he didn't go ahead with the new will? He was talking about it the last time I saw him. Asked some questions about the trickier bits in his last will. I answered them, but I was too sick to draw up a new document."

"Thank you, sir," Frank said. From the sound of it, Collingwood hadn't heard about Laurel Kenway's death. He decided to leave things that way. "I think you've told us what we needed to know."

"I should thank *you,"* Collingwood said with a smile. "It's not often I have my head patted by an attractive young lady. Unless she's a nurse or a relative."

Smiling, the three teens left the intensive care unit. But Frank's smile faded as they headed down the hall. "A new will. This changes everything. At the very least, it's a new motive to consider—if one heir knew about the will and the others didn't."

"Especially if that heir knew who got what," Nancy added.

"So, first we've got to find out if anybody knew about a new will. Then we have to see if we can find the thing," Joe said.

"I guess I'll get back on the phone to Buff," Nancy said. "Since I'll be out in Orbeck, Buff and I will handle the search there. That leaves you guys to handle the town house."

"Which means we'll need the key," Frank said. "When you talk to Buff maybe you can make arrangements to get it for us."

Nancy nodded. "Will do."

Half an hour later, they met at the Bellamy town house. Frank looked up at the windows. They were as tall as the doors in many houses Frank had seen. One thing was sure, he thought, if Stafford Bellamy had wanted to hide something, he had lots of places to do it in there.

"Oh, look," Nancy said. Set into the pavement beside the front steps was a thin wrought-iron statue of a little dog. "What's this for?"

"It's a mud-scraper," Buff explained. "Way back when, you'd put your foot on the dog's back to scrape the soles of your boots clean."

"Amazing," Nancy said as Buff gave the key to the Hardys. "I guess we'll leave you guys to it," she said to Frank and Joe. Then she and Buff left.

"Where do we start?" Joe asked, standing in the entrance hall.

"We'll take it once over lightly," Frank replied. "Check the obvious places. If that doesn't do it, we'll go room by room."

He walked inside and found himself facing the high-ceilinged front parlor of the house. It was the murder scene. One wall was dominated by a shield beautifully painted with the Bellamy crest. Surrounding it was a collection of weapons from the Middle Ages.

"Impressive," Frank said. "Some of this stuff you'd only see in museums."

Joe gave him a look. "And when did you become an expert on what the well-dressed knight in armor wears?"

"It's part of that special history project I'm doing for school—warfare from 1066 to 1914." Frank pointed at the weapons on the wall. "Most of this comes about three hundred years into what we're researching."

Joe turned away to examine the floor. "Looks like there used to be a rug here," he said.

Frank pointed to an empty set of brackets on the wall. "Guess that makes sense." He reached toward the empty space, swung round, seized Joe by the throat, and stabbed him with an imaginary blade.

Joe knocked his hand away. "Don't *do* that."

They started their search, looking first in the file drawers and desk in a room Stafford Bellamy had apparently used as an office. No luck.

"Looks like we'll have to go about this the hard way," Frank said.

"You said it," Joe replied, staring through the doorway into the next room.

Frank joined him and sighed. It was a library with several thousand books—the perfect place to hide a few pieces of paper. "We'll have to go through every one."

After hours of searching the library, the boys decided to get something to eat. They returned to their hotel—and found Brenda Carlton sitting in the lobby. "It took me six phone calls to find out where you were staying," she said. "I thought maybe you'd like to take me out for dinner." She gave Joe a flirtatious look. "And there are some new clubs down on South Street I'd like to check out."

Frank shrugged in defeat. Brenda was blackmailing them into entertaining her. But maybe it was better to keep her around rather than have her following them. They walked to Brenda's hotel, the Barclay, right on Rittenhouse Square.

After Brenda had changed, they went out looking for a restaurant. Their route took them right past the Bellamy town house.

Frank elbowed Joe in the ribs. There was a light on in the house—and they hadn't left it on.

"What are you guys doing?" Brenda demanded as they suddenly turned toward the town house.

"This is the murder scene, and there's somebody in there," Frank said. He was about to pull out the key, but then he stopped. Brenda would have a million questions if he did that. "Joe, check the roof and the servants' exit," he said. Then he rang the bell.

Frank thought the intruder would run. The last

thing he expected was for the front door to open. Cris Bellamy stood in the doorway, looking as surprised as Frank felt.

"I know you," Cris said. "Frank—Hardy, isn't it?" He glanced out toward the sidewalk. "And there's your brother. That girl—is she Nancy Drew? I read in the newspapers that she's working with the Vidocq Society as well."

"That's right," Brenda said boldly, stepping up to shake hands. "I'm Nancy Drew. Her eyes challenged Frank to say anything different. "And you're—?"

"Cris Bellamy," the young man said, taking her hand. "Buff's brother."

"And just as handsome," Brenda purred. "We saw lights on in the murder scene and thought we should check it out. Actually, we were going out for dinner and to check out the clubs on South Street. Perhaps you could suggest a place—and join us?"

"And here I was hoping for a cheesesteak," Joe grumbled. "Looks like we'll never get one."

"Come to Philadelphia and not have a cheesesteak?" Cris said. "No way. I know the best places in south Philly. They're down by Passyunk Avenue—and that's only four blocks from South Street."

They went back to Brenda's hotel, got her rental car, and drove south. They were soon in the city's Italian district. The houses were modest, but there were cars everywhere. Brenda finally found a parking space. They had to walk several blocks. When Cris pointed out their destination, Brenda stopped flirting with him and her jaw fell. "*That's* where we're eating?"

Although the neon radiance of Philadelphia's newest additions to the skyline glowed in the distance, Pat's King of Steaks seemed to belong to another world. It looked more like a fast-food sandwich shop than a restaurant. A line of people stood at two windows, ordering steak sandwiches and picking up soft drinks. The only seating was a collection of outdoor picnic-style tables.

"Guess it's not as elegant as she was expecting," Frank muttered to his brother.

"We'll grab a table," Cris announced. "You guys can order. Just ask for four cheesesteaks, *with*—which means you'll get them with onions. That okay with you, Nancy?"

Brenda smiled dreamily up at the handsome young man. "Any way you like it," she said.

Frank and Joe stepped to the end of the line. "I don't know which is worse," Joe complained. "Her flirting or her stupid little reporter's questions."

"What worries me is the way Cris is pumping her for information on the investigation," Frank said unhappily. "Either he's going to discover she's not Nancy, or Brenda is going to spill everything Nancy told her."

The line moved quickly, and they soon had the sandwiches. Frank moved to the next window for soft drinks. "Hey, they've got birch beer," he said in surprise. "Want one, Joe? Joe?"

His brother had stopped at a nearby counter loaded with condiments. "Maybe this will get her mind off Cris," Joe said. He had one of the sandwiches unwrapped and was ladling a thin red sauce over the cheesesteak. Frank peered at the canister as Joe replaced the thick wooden spoon. It was labeled hot sauce.

Joe rewrapped the sandwich, and after they paid for their food, they headed for the table that Cris and Brenda had staked out. The couple was laughing together. Frank worried about how much information the older Bellamy brother had charmed out of Brenda. "I got birch beer for everyone," he said, putting waxed cups on the table.

"And here are our cheesesteaks." Joe handed out the sandwiches.

Brenda looked dubiously at the concoction on the long roll but finally took a bite. Her face went bright red. She coughed, sputtered, then gulped her large drink. It didn't seem to help.

"Nancy, are you all right?" Cris asked.

"Yes, Nancy," Frank added in mock concern. "What's wrong?"

Brenda was still coughing as she clutched her throat. "Burns," she gasped in a strangled voice.

Cris sniffed her sandwich and coughed himself. "This is loaded with hot sauce!"

"Sure," Joe said. "I put some on all our cheesesteaks. Figured it was the Philadelphia thing to do." He took Brenda's sandwich and bit into the other end. "See?" he said. "No problem."

But even though he was prepared, Joe's face went red, too, and his voice was a little hoarse.

Brenda glared at the Hardys. "You—you—you guys!" she spluttered. Brenda finished her birch beer in one long swig, slammed the cup down, jumped up from the table, then headed down the street.

"Nancy?" Cris called.

Brenda didn't even glance back.

Frank glanced at Joe. "Oh, well," he said. "Dumped again."

In Orbeck, Nancy flew out of what used to be Stafford Bellamy's study, nearly crashing into Buff. "You didn't mention there was another door leading in there," she whispered.

Lawrence Harleigh came out the door a moment later, a nasty smile on his face. "Looking for something in particular?" he asked. "I don't think Mr. Bellamy left much cash around."

Nancy bit her lip. She hoped that Lawrence hadn't actually caught her looking in the desk. "I was trying to find an envelope. Thought I'd drop a line to my folks."

"This is an old-fashioned girl, Buff. She'd

rather write than run up our phone bill." Though Lawrence's words sounded like a compliment, his suspicion shone through.

Nancy and Buff stepped through a pair of french doors to get outside. Glancing back, she saw Lawrence staring after them.

"This is just great," Nancy muttered. "We spent the afternoon searching your uncle's library with nothing to show for it. Then your sister comes home before we could get to his bedroom. And the study turns out to have too many entrances for you to guard. Is there *anyplace* we can check tonight without being interrupted?"

Buff nodded toward the old stables. "How about Fort Bellamy? Uncle Stafford spent a lot of time there."

They came in through Stafford Bellamy's renovated war room. The ranks of soldiers still stood undisturbed. Nancy noticed a faint coating of dust on the battlelines. She turned to the shelves of warriors, paying special attention to the ones up by the ceiling. "Nothing here," she reported. "But then, this is all too open."

Buff's hand brushed against the wall as he motioned toward the unused section of the stables. "There are lots of hiding places in here." He rubbed his fingers, trying to get slivers of wood off. "Even if the place is crumbling around the edges."

Nancy stepped into the musty larger room.

"You check the stalls. I'll check the hayloft." She rested her foot on the first rung of the wooden ladder that led to the hayloft. It crumbled under her weight. "Um, want to give me a boost?"

Buff bent low and laced his fingers together. Nancy placed her toe in the cup his hands made. Between his powerful heave and her jump, she almost flew into the hayloft.

The smell of spoiled hay was much stronger here. Glancing upward, Nancy could see the stars through holes in the roof. No wonder all the hay bales had gone bad. It had been raining up here for years!

There was no way Stafford Bellamy would leave important papers up there. Disappointed, Nancy headed back to the ladder. The decaying wood under her feet sagged alarmingly.

Suddenly there was a loud groaning sound. Nancy tried to step back—but the wooden floor beneath her disintegrated.

She had time for one cry as she dropped.

Chapter Sixteen

NANCY FRANTICALLY SNATCHED for something, *anything,* to break her fall. Her hands clutched the rough edge of a thick board. Splinters tore into her palms, then the piece of wood cracked. Part of it sprang loose, almost whipping into Nancy's eye. She jerked her head around, so the jagged splinter sliced across her cheek.

Nancy lost her grip. Was the floor made of dirt, or was it concrete? It could mean the difference between a bone-jarring landing or a cracked skull.

Instead, she tumbled down into a strong pair of arms. "Wha—what?" she mumbled, staring up into Buff Bellamy's concerned face.

"I came running when I heard the floor give

way," he told her. "It's lucky you managed to hold on till I got into catching range."

"Buff?" Gwen Bellamy's sharp voice came from the war room. "Are you in here?"

Before Buff could put Nancy down, his sister appeared in the doorway. She stood silhouetted in the light of the room behind her, and Nancy wasn't sure what the young woman could see. If Gwen spotted the bleeding cut on her cheek . . .

There was only one way to hide it. Nancy turned her head, resting her wounded cheek against Buff's chest.

Gwen's eyes must have caught the movement in the darkness because she gave a little gasp. "Sorry to—*interrupt* you," Buff's older sister said coldly. "I just wanted you to know that Lawrence and I will be leaving early tomorrow morning."

Gwen turned around to stride off. Then she stopped to say, "I'll be staying at Rittenhouse Square for a few days. Preparations for the wedding. Cris went on ahead to air the place out." She regarded Buff coldly. "Not that you'd care."

There were so many feelings underlying Gwen's words, Nancy thought. Not just her dislike for "Mandy" or her annoyance at finding the two of them apparently making out. Gwen was throwing Cris in Buff's face for his willingness to help her.

Nancy's feelings, however, were much simpler. Pure worry. "Um, when did Cris leave?" she asked.

"Right after dinner," Gwen replied. "He wanted to pick up a few papers from his office. He said he'd stop by the town house on the way."

Nancy allowed herself a sigh of relief. If Cris had left after dinner, he'd be at the town house by now. Well, there hadn't been any phone calls about the Hardys' break-in.

But an idea began to percolate in her head. "I thought Cris was going to be out here tomorrow."

Gwen gave her an unfriendly look. "He will be—he'll be back tonight. But he needs to go over those papers before a Monday meeting."

Nancy nodded, deep in thought. With Gwen and Lawrence gone, that meant Cris Bellamy was the only obstacle to a full-scale search of the Orbeck estate.

She waited until Gwen had left the stables, then turned to Buff. "We'll call Frank and Joe at their hotel and tell them to come here in the morning. Is there someplace off the grounds where I can get Cris to take me?"

Buff looked a little jealous. "Why do you want Cris— Oh. You'll get him out of the way so the guys can search." His eyebrows rose as he looked at Nancy. "Are you so sure you can get him to take you?"

Nancy gave him her best flirtatious Mandy

Dean laugh. "I can make a really good try," she said. "We'll just tell the boys to wait at the gate until you wave them in."

The next morning Frank pulled up the rental car on the road outside the Bellamy estate. He and Joe had a clear view of the gray stone gateposts. Almost as soon as they stopped, they saw Buff Bellamy appear from behind one of the posts. He beckoned them in.

"Looks like Nancy got the older brother out of the way," Joe said.

"Yeah." Frank couldn't help his grumpy tone. "I wish Nancy hadn't put herself in the middle of this."

Joe grinned. "You're jealous."

Frank twisted the key in the ignition again. "Let's get going. We'll have enough work to do. You could fit three of those town houses into this dump."

He braked at the gateway, and Buff hopped aboard. "Straight ahead," he said. "I think Nancy was very optimistic thinking we could search the whole house in one day."

"Did you get anything done last night?" Frank asked.

"Just a quick look in my uncle's study. We were looking around the old stables, but we got interrupted."

"That's where we'll start then," Frank said. "And carefully this time."

Buff took them in by way of the war room. Joe whistled at the display of toy soldiers. "Hey, Frank, you should know all about this. Looks like he's got every army from history on these shelves."

Buff smiled. "Uncle Stafford loved military history. He'd always drag in references to it in his business. I remember him once telling Laurel her future was as safe as if the British army were guarding it."

Frank stood over the sand table, frowning. He suddenly turned to Buff. "When did your uncle say that?"

Buff looked a little surprised. "It was one of the last times I saw him before he died. I guess that's why it stuck in my mind."

Frank's eyes burned into Buff's. "The exact words, if you can recall them."

Buff bit his lip, trying to remember. "Not long before his death, my uncle began to get on Laurel's case about her choice of a career. He wanted her to take business courses for some reason. They'd argue about it. This time, Uncle Stafford said something like, 'My dear, if you won't worry about your future, I have. You'll be glad someday. It's as safe as if the British army—"

Then Buff shook his head. "No, he said it was safeguarded by the British army."

Frank said, "Or did he say it was safe—guarded by the British army?"

He pointed toward the battlefield. "This is the battle of Waterloo. I recognized the British squares. This is the fortified farm of La Haye Sainte. This is the town and ridge of Mont St. Jean. And this long, thin hill here—it shouldn't exist. I've copied maps, I've even studied computer simulations of the battle. I've never seen this hill or those troops."

He thrust his hand into the nonhistorical hill, jiggling the line of soldiers aside. "There's something in here!"

When Frank removed his hand, he clutched what looked like a plastic-wrapped tube. He stripped off the wrapping and found several pieces of rolled-up paper.

"What—?" Buff cried.

Frank was devouring the paper with his eyes. Joe joined him. "It's a will," he announced. "Dated shortly before Stafford Bellamy died."

Joe skipped ahead to the last page. "And it was witnessed by Hugh and Barbara Owen, Bellamy's live-in servants."

"They died with him in the car crash," Frank said. "That's why there was no word of this new will."

He held up the papers. "Which is too bad. On the first page, Stafford Bellamy admits that he's the one who made Bellamy and Kenway's money disappear. He did it to save his own land with the help of Richard Tacey. Walter Kenway was innocent. On the second page, he tries to make up for his theft by leaving most of his estate to Laurel Kenway."

Joe whirled on Buff Bellamy, seizing the front of his shirt. "You *knew* about this, didn't you? I bet you tried to suck up to Laurel when you found out what she was getting. That would let you marry your way into most of your uncle's money. But she didn't want anything to do with you, so you killed her!"

Frank expected Buff to blow up and sock his brother. Instead, the big athlete sagged in Joe's grasp.

"That's not what happened." Buff's voice was full of pain. "I loved Laurel. We went out for a year—her first year in college. We wanted to get married after she graduated. Gwen found out—and she wouldn't hear of me marrying 'a bricklayer's daughter.' That's how Mr. Kenway started out in business. For Gwen, it was worse than him being a jailbird, although she threw that in Laurel's face, too."

"It sounds like something changed your mind, though," Frank said.

Buff nodded. "Gwen got help from Uncle Stafford. He told me it 'wouldn't do' for me to marry Laurel. It was all right for him to go into business with her father, but she couldn't marry into our family!"

Joe glared at Buff, not buying his story. "If you loved Laurel, why didn't you tell your uncle to take a hike?"

Buff stared at the floor. "This was back when I was still racing. It costs money to keep a boat and a maintenance crew. My uncle was paying the bills. He threatened to cut off the flow of money. And I—" His voice got hoarse. "I caved in. I broke up with Laurel and started doing some heavy partying—trying to forget."

Buff looked as if he had just tasted something disgusting. "Gwen blamed me—and the arguments—when my uncle had a mild heart attack a little over two years ago. I think he regretted his snobbishness then, but it was too late. I was a playboy now, and Laurel thought I had all the backbone of a jellyfish. Maybe she was right. But I *didn't* kill her. And if I knew about a will that just about disinherited me, why would I help you guys find it?"

Joe had no answer for that. But Frank headed out for the car. "Let's see if we can find Richard Tacey," he said.

The executive was doing some weekend work at his office. His face went gray when he saw the will.

"You found it" was all he could say.

Frank leaned across Tacey's desk. "So you knew about the new will."

Tacey nodded, licking his lips nervously. "Mr. Bellamy had two heart attacks before the final one. He recovered, but he was very moody. I think nearly dying got his conscience working overtime. He called me out to the Orbeck mansion and said he'd figured out a way to confess to everything after his death."

"Through his will," Frank said.

Tacey nodded. "That was fine for him, but what about me?"

"What's your problem?" Joe demanded. "It's more than seven years since the fraud. You couldn't be arrested."

"Think what it would do to the firm—to my good name," Tacey said. "I argued with Mr. Bellamy, but his mind was made up."

Tacey looked down at his trembling hands. "When Mr. Bellamy died, I was in a complete panic. But the will never turned up."

"Well, you weren't going to talk about it, were you?" Joe mocked.

"I did tell one person," Tacey admitted. "I figured he ought to know about it, since he'd be the one inheriting the company."

Frank was so far over Tacey's desk, he was nearly nose to nose with the man. "You told Cris Bellamy?" he demanded. "When?"

"I'll never forget it," Tacey said. "I told him the night Laurel Kenway was murdered."

Chapter Seventeen

"I KNOW WHAT YOU'RE THINKING," Buff Bellamy said in the elevator going down from Tacey's office. "And you can't be right. Cris would never—"

Joe hardly heard him with the upsetting thoughts that were swirling in his mind. He was thinking of M-O-M. Not his mother, but the three building blocks of any murder case. Motive. Opportunity. Means.

Cris Bellamy had motive. If he had learned that his uncle's new will gave Laurel Kenway the lion's share of the Bellamy money, that would have been motive enough to kill her.

As for opportunity . . . the gleaming office tower that housed Bellamy Holdings was just a few minutes' walk from Rittenhouse Square.

Cris even had an alibi. He'd been working with Richard Tacey, a man who had serious reasons of his own not to mention the will.

And when it came to means, well, Cris Bellamy lived in his uncle's town house. He was all too familiar with the weapons collection. Maybe he'd even handled that knife before.

Joe hated to admit it, but a pretty good case could now be made against Cris Bellamy.

Great, he thought. We've got everything but proof.

The elevator doors opened. Buff and the boys had crossed the lobby and were almost at the door when Joe spotted a familiar face on one of the newspapers in the lobby newsstand. It was Nancy Drew on her rearing horse.

For a second, Joe thought the paper was *Truth Weekly.* Then, with a sick feeling, he realized it was a local Philadelphia daily.

"Frank," he said, pointing.

Frank Hardy flew over to the newsstand and bought a copy of the paper. He opened it, began reading, then looked up, his face a mask of fury.

"So much for Little Miss Journalistic Integrity," Frank growled. "This is a wire story, picked up from *Today's Times,* with Brenda's byline. She doesn't just identify Nancy as the girl in this picture. Brenda must have faxed everything to River Heights last night. She's spilled the 'exclusive story' on *why* Nancy was posing as Buff's companion. Our undercover operation is not exactly a secret anymore."

"I guess maybe she was mad at us," Joe said. "Or Daddy made her give him everything she had."

"Here." Frank tossed the newspaper at Buff, then stalked toward the pay phones. "I'm just going to have a word with the star reporter."

But after a few moments on the phone, he hung up in disgust. "Brenda checked out. She must be off to the airport already."

Buff was still holding the newspaper Frank had dumped in his hands. "This paper gets delivered to our place out in Orbeck," he said uneasily. "I barely pay attention, except to read the sports pages. Cris is usually up the earliest. He grabs the paper as soon as it arrives. . . ." His voice died away.

"So Cris must know who Nancy is," Frank said, horror creeping into his voice.

"Hey, calm down," Joe told his brother.

"I'm trying," Frank said. "But I keep remembering what happened when we paid a visit to Cris Bellamy—our interesting elevator ride. Cris is an engineer. He'd know how to sabotage the hoist. And who else knew we were there?"

The color slowly left Joe's face as he recalled their lunch with Cris. Ed Fitzgibbon had really been pounding away at the older Bellamy brother. Then Cris managed to escape, pleading a business emergency. A little while later, when the Hardys and the murder investigator got on the elevator, it had dropped like a rock.

"I thought Cris looked calm enough when Fitzgibbon questioned him," Joe insisted. Even he realized he was just trying to reassure himself.

"Calm on the outside, maybe," Frank said, his voice full of worry. "But I think Cris is running scared. He handled the murder all right—even cold-bloodedly. I mean, he even stashed the knife in Buff's car to shift the blame."

Buff looked unhappy as Frank spoke, but he didn't say anything.

"But I think his first taste of what a real police interrogation would be like shook Cris up," Frank continued. "Fitzgibbon had Cris on the defensive only seconds into the interview."

He turned to Joe. "You remember how evasive Cris got?"

"He trotted out his nice little alibi, and Fitzgibbon started knocking holes in it," Joe had to admit. "Cris began to get worried."

"I don't care about that," Frank said. "What bothers me is the way Cris chose to end his worry—gimmicking that elevator." He took a deep breath, then finally put into words what was concerning them all. "What if he tries to do something to Nancy?"

"Cris had his chance when that chimney

nearly fell on Nancy," Joe said. "And he *saved* her, remember?"

But the worried look wasn't leaving his brother's face. "That was before he knew Nancy was working undercover. He'll know that now."

Frank frowned. "In fact, he may have started suspecting her. Remember how he went after Brenda? Asking if she was Nancy Drew?"

"Then he must have been confused when she claimed that she was," Joe said with a laugh.

But Frank's mood didn't lighten. "Well, he won't be confused now. He'll probably think we tried to put something over on him. I just hope he doesn't take it out on Nancy."

Joe jammed his hands in his pockets and stared at the floor. "If Nancy really is out there in trouble, I'll be the guilty one," he said in a small voice. "It will all be my fault."

"What are you talking about?" Frank demanded.

"The leaks," Joe said miserably. "Remember all the things you couldn't figure about the leaks? Who had so much information about what we were investigating? Who knew so much about the investigators—like about the bad blood between Brenda and Nancy?"

He could feel both Frank's and Buff's eyes on him now.

"There was somebody right beside you all the time. You never suspected, but you should have." Joe's chest was tight as he tried to draw breath for what he had to say. *"I'm* the leak, guys. I was trying to shut down this investigation from the start. First, I called the local newspapers, figuring the last thing the Vidocq people wanted was a media circus. Then, I decided to target Nancy."

Frank winced at Joe's choice of words.

"I mean," Joe went on desperately, "I called Brenda Carlton, thinking she might be able to get Nancy off the case. But then Nancy got her picture in the paper, and things got out of hand."

"That's why you were so quiet when we went to meet Brenda with Nancy," Frank recalled. He suddenly stabbed a finger against Joe's chest. "And why you were being such a nice guy when I questioned that bartender."

Joe nodded. "I knew he was innocent."

"You nearly got me killed when he panicked and pulled that gun," Frank said angrily. He took a deep breath to calm down. "At least that explains some of the stuff that's been screwing us up. The only thing I don't understand is how you tipped off those mob guys to crush Stafford Bellamy's limo."

Joe stared. "I didn't tip them off," he said. "How would I know who to call?"

"One person knew we were looking into Mr. Bellamy's death," Frank said slowly. "Cris. We mentioned it at lunch."

"But how would he—" Joe started to ask, then answered his own question. "I think somebody said it along the way. Organized crime types turn up in junkyards, in the service industries—"

"And in construction," Frank finished. "That gives us another thread of circumstantial evidence. But we can wait on that. Our main concern right now has to be Nancy."

He turned to Buff. "Where did she go off with Cris this morning?"

The athlete still seemed in a state of shock. Joe felt a little sorry for him. First they'd accused his brother of murder, then Joe's confession had rocked the guy. When Buff recovered, he might feel like punching Joe's head in. The way Joe felt right now, he might let him.

"They drove down to the Delaware River," Buff finally said. "My uncle had some riverfront property down there. It's where I left my boat and my uncle's seaplane. Cris and Mandy—I mean, Nancy—were going out in my boat."

Joe glanced at his brother, then back at Buff. "The seaplane—does it run?"

"Sure," Buff said. "I'd go down there every once in a while just to crank things over. I can't fly, but I could start the engine."

"Well, Frank's got a pilot's license. Let's get down to this property and get that seaplane into the air. We've got to find your boat—and Nancy—before Cris does something stupid."

Joe dashed through the revolving doors of the office building without looking back at the other two. He was too busy trying to ignore the accusing little voice in the back of his head.

If anything happens to Nancy, it will be your fault, the voice said. *Your fault, Joe.*

Chapter Eighteen

"THIS IS SOME BOAT!" Nancy yelled over to Cris Bellamy.

She wasn't sure he heard. Cris was driving Buff's racing boat up the Delaware River fast enough to cause a slipstream. Besides seriously ruffling her hair, the whipping breeze gave her an idea of their speed. So did the deep-throated roar of the engines. They made the floor under her feet throb with power. She could feel the vibration all through her body, and her heart seemed to speed up with every push Cris gave the throttle.

The only drawback that Nancy could see was that the two-person racer had separate cockpits. One was for steering, the other for operating the engines. Buff's place as the boat's captain was an empty space between and behind the two consoles. Today Cris was controlling everything from the left-hand cockpit.

As she watched his long, slim fingers deftly direct the controls, she wondered how much practice Cris had. She couldn't ask, though. Conversation could be carried on only in a scream, and Nancy wasn't about to scream.

At last Cris pulled back on the throttle. The throbbing of the engines receded to a distant thunder. "We're getting into traffic," he explained. "This is the Philadelphia waterfront."

They passed a beautiful promenade and marina. Piers had been converted to restaurants. Nancy saw a tall ship tied up at one dock and an old-fashioned battleship moored at another.

A colorfully painted boat shot across their bows. "A water taxi," Cris explained. "They take passengers back and forth between Philadelphia and Camden, on the New Jersey side of the river."

Nancy noticed that Cris was reaching into the well of the cockpit, down by his feet. He came up with a lifejacket and a safety helmet. She looked down by her feet. Nothing there. Maybe under the seat . . .

As she shifted, Cris glanced over, buckling on his helmet. "I'm afraid you won't find anything, Nancy."

There was just a fire extinguisher . . . wait. He'd called her "Nancy" instead of "Mandy."

Had she misheard? Then Nancy caught the look Cris was sending her way. "I'm afraid your secret is out," Cris said. "There was a front-page story here in town. Your reporter friend from River Heights wired quite a scoop home." He gave her a smile without a trace of laughter in it. "I think I met her last night. She claimed to be you and tried to pump me for information—not as well as *you* did, though."

Nancy did her best to keep her voice calm. "I was wondering a lot earlier if someone in the Orbeck house might not be onto me. I mean, after that chimney fell down."

"A complete accident, as far as I know. If I'd suspected you then, I wouldn't have been so heroic."

"Well, I appreciated it," Nancy said. "At the time."

"It was only later that I realized you were oh-so-quietly asking questions of everybody. I should have wondered more about you. Buff's never gotten over Laurel."

"So Laurel was Buff's 'last serious romance'?" Nancy asked. "At least those were your sister's words."

"Still asking questions?" Cris may have been trying to keep a light tone, but Nancy heard the ring of iron in his words. "If you had to ask that one, you don't know as much as I thought."

"What do you mean?" Nancy shot back.

"It all began with Uncle Stafford's will," Cris

said. "By the way, his death was just as it seemed—an accident that occurred while he was being rushed to the hospital. When I heard the Vidocq Society was looking into it, I arranged to get the wrecked limo destroyed. I figured that would make the accident look like a murder and distract you."

"It nearly did," Nancy admitted, remembering the arguments over organized crime. "How'd you manage to get rid of the limo so quickly?"

"Real estate means dealing with construction people," Cris said with a shrug. "Some are connected to the mob. A guy who owed me a favor called a friend who called another friend."

"Well, your goodfella network demolished the car just as we got there," Nancy said.

"Not that it stopped you people." Cris's tone was grim. "You came sniffing around in Orbeck. The Hardys turned up at Bellamy Holdings again. That weakling Tacey was beginning to sweat."

"That's not a nice way to talk about your boss," Nancy said.

"But soon I'll be *his* boss," Cris pointed out. "If all goes well."

"I wouldn't bet on it." Nancy did her best to sound confident, not easy when she was still shouting over the breeze. "The whole reason I got you out here was to get a team into the mansion to search for your uncle's new will."

Cris turned to her again, his lips curling in a

bitter smile. "I wish them luck. They'll have a day. I've spent *months* looking for that stupid piece of paper, just to destroy it. My uncle had two big libraries, one in each house. Thousands of books, and I've been over every page of them. I've been in the attic at Orbeck and in the cellar of the Rittenhouse Square place. I've traced every key my uncle owned, in case there was a safe-deposit box somewhere. I even persuaded Tacey to have the safe in my uncle's office broken open. And I found nothing!"

He slammed his fist onto the edge of the cockpit. "Half the time I wondered how my uncle had rearranged our inheritance. The rest of the time, I just dreamed of burning the thing."

Cris gave Nancy a sour look. "If only Gwen had had the sense to leave well enough alone! Laurel might have been married to Buff by now. Knowing Buff, he'd have tried to share the wealth. Maybe he could even have persuaded Laurel to hush up my uncle's idiot confession. But no." He spat the words. "Gwen had to play the snob. She got my uncle to break things up between Buff and Laurel. So what if she made Laurel hate us all?"

"When did you find out about the new will?" Nancy asked.

"It's something I didn't mention in my alibi," Cris replied. "I was working late with Tacey, getting things ready for a meeting with our lawyers the next day. He got me in his office and asked if I'd found any other documents Uncle Stafford might have left around. Finally he stopped beating around the bush and told me that he suspected my uncle had made a new will."

Cris gave a short, sharp laugh. "That was a shock, I can tell you. But it got worse. Uncle wanted to confess his ancient wrongdoing and clear Walter Kenway's name. How nice for Uncle Stafford!" he said sarcastically. "But," he continued, "that meant the company I'm supposed to inherit—that I've spent most of my life learning how to run—will go straight on the trash heap. And the Bellamy name—*my* name—will be remembered for some shabby little fraud that happened before I was ten years old."

His hands were so tight on the steering gear, he looked ready to tear it off.

Nancy felt cold, and it wasn't the breeze whipping off the river. "Was it worth a murder to stop that from happening?"

Cris kept his eyes straight ahead. "I didn't mean to do anything," he said. "I just had this need to go and talk to Laurel. So I sneaked out of the office—not too difficult, really. I walked over to Rittenhouse Square. Laurel was alone, and I asked a few questions. I only wanted to find out if she knew anything about this will."

"And?" Nancy prompted.

"Little Laurel was a lot brighter than any of us gave her credit for. She figured out what I was after from the questions I asked. Of course, she'd had hints. Even as a child, she remembered that her father denied stealing any money. And after his illness, I think Uncle Stafford dropped a clue here and there, talking about the fraud."

"So what did Laurel do?"

"She laughed right in my face," Cris said tightly. "She said she hoped there *was* a will, because now she'd be searching high and low for it. She didn't care about money or the inheritance. She just hoped Uncle Stafford was man enough to admit what he'd done. If he had, she said she'd take great delight in dragging the Bellamy name through the mud."

Cris's lips were as tight as his grip on the wheel. Each word came through as if it were causing him pain. "I asked her not to do that, but Laurel said she owed us nothing. My uncle had betrayed her father. Gwen treated her like a servant, Lawrence chased her, I ignored her, and Buff—Buff broke her heart.

"This girl, a daughter of a mere bricklayer, was going to do her best to ruin us. I couldn't allow that. She was jeering at me, following me across the room to the museum wall. That's what we called the wall decorated with great-grandfather's medieval collection. Everything seemed very clear, as if I'd already planned it. I saw the knife on the wall and took it. One hand on her throat, to choke off the awful things she was saying. And then—one stab."

Cris shuddered so badly, Nancy feared he'd lose control of the boat. Then they steadied out, although his voice didn't.

"She—she didn't die immediately. Laurel fumbled with the knife, staring at me with these eyes . . ." His voice died away.

When Cris spoke again, his voice was like the clang of iron. "She had to die, Nancy. Just as you have to die."

Nancy forced herself to face the murderer. "You'll never get away with it, you know." Even she was surprised at how calm her voice sounded. "There's evidence against you, besides your confession or your uncle's will." She leaned far out of her cockpit to point at his hands. "You left marks as distinct as fingerprints when you half-strangled Laurel to death. Long, thin bruises, from a long, slim hand. Buff's hand doesn't look anything like that. It's all in the medical examiner's report. Sooner or later, someone will notice."

"I'll take my chances," Cris replied. "Since it seems you didn't notice this damning evidence until it was too late."

His eyes went back to scan the river. "In a few miles, things get a little tricky. You can lose the main channel of the river and possibly hang up your boat."

Cris gave her an icy smile. "Very dangerous, if the boat is going too fast." He shoved the throttle, and the boat leaped forward.

Spray whipped into Nancy's face. They were moving much too fast for her to jump overboard.

"Oh, your friends may be suspicious," Cris called over the engines' roar. "But the crash will just look like an accident. I'll be taking as much of a chance as you—well, almost. You shouldn't have refused to wear your safety gear. I'll be very sad when I tell everyone."

His face went blank as he turned forward again. But even though he was muttering, Nancy caught his words.

"With luck, Nancy, you'll scarcely feel a thing."

Chapter Nineteen

THE CONTROLS OF THE SEAPLANE felt alien under Frank Hardy's fingers. The aircraft seemed sluggish in responding to his commands—especially for more speed.

Maybe it was just Frank's reaction to getting into the air. Anything would seem slow after their wild drive through Philadelphia with Joe at the wheel and Buff shouting directions. They'd come to a screeching halt at the Bellamy property, which included a "cottage" that could have swallowed the Hardy home back in Bayport twice over, a huge boathouse, and a sort of marine hangar that housed the seaplane.

Joe came into the hangar after checking out the cottage. "Fresh dishes for two in the drainer—they haven't even dried off yet. Looks like they had a leisurely brunch first."

Frank was topping off the airplane's gas tanks from a private pump, then he rushed through the usual preflight checklist. Buff appeared in the hangar, his face pale.

"I just checked the boathouse," he said. "There's good news and bad news. They took my racing boat, not the cabin cruiser, which means Cris had to spend more time setting it up."

"What's the bad news?" Joe asked as he helped Frank run down the safety checks.

"It's easy to fake an accident on a muscle boat." Buff looked truly worried. Frank guessed he'd finally accepted that Cris was the guilty party. "It's a light hull with an overpowered engine. A disaster looking to happen."

Joe gave him a look. "And you raced these for fun?"

With the checks finished, Frank ordered the others on board and radioed in his flight plan. "We'll be heading upstream on the river." Buff had suggested that this direction was a better bet for faking a crash.

Frank jockeyed the ungainly craft into the air, flying as low as he dared over the busy river traffic. As he manipulated the controls, he repeated one thought like a mantra. *We go faster than that boat. We go faster than that boat.*

In spite of his hopes, they were well upstream

of the Philadelphia waterfront when Buff suddenly pointed from the copilot's seat. "There! There she is!"

"You're sure?" Frank yelled over the heavy drone of the engines.

"I can recognize my own boat," Buff said a little huffily.

Frank first spotted a white wake on the river. As he circled, he saw a long, low hull built to cut through the water. Two cockpits appeared in the rear of the boat. A guy in a safety helmet and life vest was in one; a young woman whose reddish blond hair trailed behind her in the breeze was in the other.

"Well, we've found them." Frank's face was grim as he stared down at the pair below. So near and yet so far. "I can keep circling—let Cris know that we're watching."

"Yeah, but he's got safety equipment up the wazoo. He could still crash the boat," Buff said.

"Suppose you buzz him?" Joe suggested. "You know, play aerial chicken."

"We might scare Cris, but we won't stop him," Frank said. "Or save Nancy. We'd be handing him the perfect excuse for any 'accident.'"

They flew on. Frank felt like an ungainly pelican lumbering after a sleek otter. The racing craft suddenly shot ahead.

"Either he's spotted us, or he's starting something." Frank's mouth was dry, but his hands were slippery as he opened the throttle.

"Take this crate down," Joe ordered, getting up from his seat in the rear of the cockpit.

"What are you doing?" Buff demanded as the younger Hardy moved toward the plane's hatch.

"It feels stuffy in here, so I thought I'd take a stroll out on the wing," Joe replied.

"Are you crazy?" Frank demanded.

"No more than usual, I hope." Joe's face was pale as he worked to open the hatch. "Bring this thing down as low as you can. Then hold her steady over the driver's seat of that boat."

Joe heaved the hatch open, and a breeze like a small gale whipped through the seaplane's cabin. Dust and some sheets of paper swirled around.

For a second, Frank had to fight to hold the plane steady.

Joe, braced in the doorway, held on to the hatch for dear life. "A little gentler, please," he yelled over the howl of incoming wind. "That bounce and roll nearly threw me out."

Frank and Buff both glanced away from the boat they were pursuing to the door. Joe was just slipping out. He gave them an airy wave. Then the hatch closed behind him.

Wind like a rushing express train hit Joe the moment he stuck his body outside the seaplane's cabin. He'd planned to brace himself between a wing strut and one of the pontoons. Instead, he was almost torn loose and hurled toward the greenish blue ribbon of river below.

Luckily, he'd managed to hook one arm around the strut. One foot hung down, the other scraped desperately against the side of the cabin.

Grunting with the exertion of just staying in place, he thought, This will teach me. The guys in the action movies always make this stuff look so easy.

His hair was blown straight back on his head, and both the arms of his shirt and the legs of his pants were flapping like flags in a stiff breeze. His eyes began to tear because of the force of the wind hitting his face.

"Great," he muttered. "I won't be able to see when the big moment comes."

The plane abruptly dipped, leaving his stomach about a thousand yards back and two thousand yards up. Joe fought to tighten his hold as the aircraft dove. He concentrated on the wing strut as he thought, Maybe I don't want to see.

Now the seaplane leveled off, and Joe could hear some competition to the drone of the aviation engine. From below came the snarl of the racing boat's power plant.

Cris Bellamy was crouched over the powerboat's controls, when either the plane's engine noise or the shadow it cast alerted him. He looked back, his eyes going big behind his racing goggles as he saw Joe hanging from the wing.

"A little farther down," Joe muttered through clenched teeth. He knew there was no way Frank could hear his instructions, unless he was psychic. But the seaplane did dip a little, picking up speed.

Joe looked down and immediately wished he hadn't. There was just the whiteness of the wake beneath him—that and the continuous spray soaking the bottoms of his jeans.

Frank had to be moving the plane's instruments micron by micron. Slowly, Joe's feet seemed to float forward. Now he could see the very rear of the boat, its propellers tearing the water. Then he saw more of the boat's body. If he dropped now, he'd bounce off the streamlined engine cover and probably land on the propellers. The result would be ground Joe.

Then, just ahead of his toes, Joe saw the back of the cockpit. "A little more . . . a *little* more," he chanted. He hung with both hands now, ready to drop.

The plane's airspeed picked up a bit. He was going to fly past. . . .

Joe let go of the strut. He dropped like an air-to-ground missile right into the open spot between the cockpits.

For a second, Joe feared he was going to go right through the bottom of the boat and sink it. Pain screamed from his feet to his hips. Wobbling, almost tumbling back onto the engines,

Joe twined both hands together and swung his arms like a giant club.

His blow caught Cris on the shoulder pad of his life jacket. And while it startled him—the boat wavered for a moment in its headlong charge across the water—the blow didn't hurt him.

Cris turned from the controls to grapple with Joe, who fell against the cockpit coaming—the raised lip that kept water out. They exchanged a flurry of blows, with Joe getting the worst of it. Getting ready to jump, Joe hadn't thought of the protective gear Cris was wearing. It didn't just defend him in a crash. With the life vest shielding his torso and the helmet on his head, Cris might as well have been a knight in armor.

Joe's punches just couldn't connect with flesh. He wasn't hurting Cris, he was just annoying him.

But when Cris threw a punch, he was doing damage. Joe had already been beaten up by the wind and by his fall. Cris slammed a couple of heavy blows into Joe's gut that nearly knocked him out of the cockpit. He tried to cover his stomach and his face.

Cris was out of his seat, now grabbing Joe by the throat, trying to strangle him. Joe managed to bat the clutching hands away. Cris hammered another punch into Joe.

The world turned black except for a small

circle of light in which Joe saw the blurred image of Cris Bellamy's goggled face. Joe's eyes had trouble focusing. The image before him wavered—the face retreated, then came closer. Joe heard a girl's voice cry out, and realized that Nancy must be trying to help him. But Cris shrugged off Nancy's blows, which fell uselessly on his padded vest. He pushed Nancy away.

Joe thrashed, trying to take advantage of Cris's distraction, but he was pinned under his opponent's body. Fuzzily, Joe realized he was now at the side of the cockpit. His head was back, the raised lip of the cockpit digging into his neck. The clouds overhead lurched wildly back and forth as the boat roared on unpiloted.

Cris Bellamy leaned over Joe. He thrust his left elbow under Joe's chin, forcing his head back even farther. Cris slid his forearm across Joe's throat. His right hand came down on his left wrist, and he began to push. If Joe didn't do something quick, he knew that Cris was going to crush his windpipe.

Joe thrust his arms up, trying to force Cris back. His hands skittered across the life vest, reached Cris's shoulders, slipped—

With a last desperate grasp, Joe managed to catch hold of the edge of the safety helmet Cris was wearing.

Cris tossed his head, trying to jar Joe's hands free, and the stranglehold on Joe's throat eased.

He managed a quick gulp of air as Cris pushed forward again.

It was a hopeless battle. Joe's arms, up and extended, couldn't hope to hold Cris off forever.

Still, the end came as a surprise. The chinstraps holding Cris's helmet on snapped, and it flew away in the breeze screaming over them.

Through the goggles he still wore, Cris's blue eyes looked mad with fury. He smacked his forehead down on Joe's face.

Joe's arms were still up in the air. There was no way for him block or even deflect the blow.

Joe seemed to see Cris from the end of a long, dark tunnel. His brain screamed orders to his hands to punch, to chop, to slam into the side of his enemy's now-naked head.

But Joe's muscles felt like pudding. His arms crept up as if he were in a slow-motion movie. His hands plucked feebly at the front of Cris's life jacket.

Joe's oxygen-starved brain could barely cling to consciousness. Launching a counterattack was completely beyond him.

But Joe was conscious enough to feel Cris Bellamy's hands twisting in the front of his shirt. In a murderous rage, the killer yanked Joe upright with no effort at all.

Joe was coughing but breathing. With every breath, the world got a little clearer. His arms still hung like lead, his fingers too weak even to grab onto Cris.

Before Joe could realize what was happening, Cris was hauling him up and out of the cockpit.

And, with the way he felt right now, Joe knew only one thing was going to happen.

He was going to sink and drown.

Chapter Twenty

JOE HUNG LIKE A DEAD WEIGHT from Cris Bellamy's fists. He gasped for breath, his head lolling back. He couldn't even face the man who was about to kill him.

From the corner of his eye, Joe caught a movement. He heard a thump. Then the grip on his shirt loosened. He collapsed back onto the pilot's seat.

Cris Bellamy slumped on top of him.

Joe felt his eyes drift closed. It would be so easy now to give in to the darkness—

"Joe! *Joe!*" an annoyed voice was yelling.

Joe cracked his eyes opened and rolled his head in the direction the shouting came from.

He saw a pretty girl with reddish blond hair blown all over her head and damp from flying spray. Didn't he know her? Of course. Nancy. Nancy Drew.

What was she shouting?

"Joe, you've got to snap out of it. You have the only working set of controls on this boat. Cris disconnected mine."

Cris . . . confused memories of the fight came back to Joe. What was Cris doing lying on top of him?

Then he remembered they were in a boat that was going to crash. Adrenaline flooded Joe's body. His heart began to thump, and his head came bolt upright. They weren't headed straight for the land. But the angle the boat took as it wallowed along would take them straight into the pilings on a pier jutting out into the water.

Joe frantically thrust Cris Bellamy out of his way as he fumbled for the controls. Back on the throttle, turn the wheel—

The sleek racing craft slewed around from Joe's clumsy attempts at control. He oversteered, cutting the wheel too much to the left, then too much to the right, trying to compensate. The boat seemed to stagger and reel across the water. The engines were almost off, but they still had a frightening amount of momentum.

They passed the edge of the pier close enough to see the faces of some very scared fishermen.

"Crazy kids!" one man yelled.

"What are they doing in that cockpit?" another asked.

Joe killed the engines, and the boat came to rest in the middle of the water. He thrust Cris Bellamy away so that the unconscious killer lay sprawled on the boat's front deck.

"Last I remember, Cris here was about to give me a crash course in swimming." Joe carefully probed the side of his face. It hurt. Everything hurt. "How did you persuade him to stop?"

Silently, Nancy held up a fire extinguisher. Her fingers were still clenched around the nozzle end of the tube in a death-grip. "I swung this as hard as I could."

Joe checked that Cris was still breathing. He was.

"Good work," Joe said. "And good aim." He shook his head and immediately regretted it.

"Are you all right?" Nancy asked.

"I hurt," Joe said. "Even worse, now that's two I owe you."

"Two you owe me?" Nancy said blankly. "Two what?"

"I'm the one who got you into this mess," Joe confessed. "I leaked all the information to the press." He gulped. "Frank was wondering who could have known about you and Brenda Carlton. I did—and I called her up in River Heights."

"You called Brenda?" Nancy looked angry enough to swing the fire extinguisher again. But this time the target would be Joe's head.

"She went home," he said, "but not before she

faxed the whole story to her dad. It's not only all over River Heights, it was picked up by the national wire services. It's everywhere."

Nancy just shrugged. "You know how newspapers are. They'll go with any freak-show kind of feature if it sells copies. But they prefer hard news." She glanced over at the unconscious Cris Bellamy. "Like capturing a murderer, for instance."

Joe still couldn't meet her eyes. "I was wrong about Buff Bellamy," he said. "And I was wrong to try to sabotage the investigation. I was just wrong about this case, period."

"Oh, I don't know," Nancy said lightly. "No case is a waste if I get to hear you apologize three times in a row. And you did your best to make things up. I couldn't believe that you'd actually jump from an airplane to a speeding powerboat to try to save me."

Joe blinked. "Now that you mention it, neither do I."

A rumble overhead caused them to look up. Frank Hardy brought the seaplane in for a perfect splashdown. Then, feathering the plane's props, he taxied the aircraft across the water to the drifting boat.

The hatch on the cabin popped open, and Buff Bellamy stuck his head out. "You guys okay?" he yelled over.

Joe winced at the shout.

Nancy called back, "We're all right." She

pointed a thumb at Cris. "Even sleeping beauty here."

"Frank's been on the radio," Buff reported. "The Philadelphia Police Marine Unit is on the way, not to mention every waterborne cop in all the towns nearby."

Soon a small fleet of powerboats was coming toward them.

"Good," Joe muttered as a policeman lifted the now-groggy Cris onto a police boat. "Maybe we can catch a ride back to town with somebody who knows how to drive one of these things."

Almost a month had passed before Frank and Joe Hardy were back in Philadelphia again. The scene was familiar. Once again, they were at the luncheon meeting of the Vidocq Society. Their host, as before, was Will Resnick. The other people at their table were familiar as well. Carson and Nancy Drew sat across from Joe and Frank. Sitting beside Nancy was Buff Bellamy.

"So, Cris confessed to everything and just pleaded guilty?" Resnick said.

"Yep," Frank said. "After being hit on the head with a fire extinguisher, I think he was actually relieved when the police showed up."

Resnick turned to Buff. "I read that Bellamy Holdings has pretty much gone under."

Buff nodded. "Basically, Bellamy Holdings has crashed since my uncle's last will was made public. His posthumous confession has destroyed the company. Also," he continued, "with the new will, the whole inheritance picture has been turned on its head. All sorts of people have turned up, claiming to be Laurel's relatives. Nobody knows how much—or little—we're going to see."

"This must be a blow to your sister," Nancy said.

"Bigger than you know—Lawrence dumped her," Buff said. "She was feeling pretty bad when I finally went to see her. But we talked. She feels everything was her fault. If she hadn't been so nasty to Laurel . . ." He let the sentence trail off. "Anyway, we are talking. And she's gone back to her job at the museum."

He gave Nancy a big grin. "And speaking of jobs, I've taken a little offer."

"I'd expect you'd have gotten offers from everywhere," Joe said.

Buff nodded. "Most of them calculated to use my recent fame, if you want to call it that. I've had enough of this monkey-in-the-zoo celebrity. A friend of mine is starting up his own boat company and needs a test pilot."

"No more racing?" Nancy asked.

"I think that part of my life is over," Buff said.

They finished lunch, then Resnick went to the podium.

"As you know, when we bring a case to a successful conclusion, we like to have a brief presentation by the investigators. In the case of

Laurel Kenway, we've gotten a lot of the basic information from reporters on our local papers—"

"Which does *not* include Brenda Carlton," Nancy said with some pleasure. "Her fame—and mine—was pretty fleeting."

"A one-day wonder," Carson Drew said, smiling.

"Now Brenda is complaining that her father pulled her out right before the scoop of her career," Nancy added.

"Couldn't have happened to a nicer girl." Frank glanced over at his brother. "What do you think, Joe?"

Joe looked nervously around the table. The bruises he'd gotten in his fight with Cris Bellamy had healed. But his ego had taken a beating, too, and he felt very self-conscious when Will Resnick invited Nancy up to the podium to speak on the case. Nancy, in turn, invited the Hardys to join her.

"Frank, Joe, and I have gotten a certain amount of publicity as the ones who captured Cris Bellamy," Nancy said. "But even though we're not official members of Vidocq, I know that my father and I have credited the society with solving this case."

Frank leaned toward the microphone. "That goes for my brother and me, as well," he said.

Joe nodded, hoping his anxiety didn't show. This was Nancy's big chance for revenge. She had him standing in front of half the members of the Vidocq Society. When she exposed him as the leak who had so hindered the investigation, the reaction of this roomful of professionals would hurt him even more than she'd been hurt.

"There's a good reason for crediting the Vidocq Society," Nancy went on. "Frank, Joe, and I aren't professionals."

Smiling, she glanced at the boys. "At least, not yet. And although we brought this case to a close in a rather—ah—"

"Unprofessional manner?" Frank suggested.

"I was going to say 'dramatic fashion,'" Nancy shot back. "But we couldn't have solved it at all without the professional expertise of many Vidocq members. Mr. Fitzgibbon's interrogation put Cris Bellamy on the run. Dr. Fell's analysis of the medical examiners' reports revealed the physical evidence that linked Cris to the crime."

"His hand matched the bruises on Laurel Kenway's throat exactly," Dr. Fell said from the audience.

"Without the help of agents Portino and Sharpe, we'd never have gotten the information about the missing will out of Mr. Tacey," Nancy added. "And many members were very generous with information about the social and financial in-groups of Philadelphia society. We thank you all."

Nancy looked down for a second, then glanced around the room. "We were lucky to solve this case. I'm very lucky to be here at all. Okay, a little luck in getting to the truth is a good thing. But for truth to beget truth, as your motto says, you need to collect some truths in the first place. That is what the society did from the beginning. And that is why this case is the Vidocq Society's success, rather than mine, Frank and Joe's, or anyone else's."

She bobbed her head slightly in response to the generous applause.

"I have just one question," Will Resnick said as the room grew quiet again. "Did you ever find out who was leaking information on the investigation?"

Joe gulped. Here it comes, he thought.

But Nancy was shaking her head. "I'm afraid we suffered from a great deal of irresponsible media interest during this case. I myself had some problems because of a freelance photographer and a less-than-professional reporter from my hometown. I suspect that a lot of people were prying, rather than just one person. Let's leave it as a mystery the society won't have to solve—"

She shot a glance around the room that somehow managed to land right on Joe.

"Unless," Nancy added, "it happens again."

Joe had lived through exploding bombs, fires, and the bullets of terrorist assassins. But he never felt more relieved than he did as he, Frank, and Nancy came down from that podium.

"I want to say thanks," he whispered to Nancy. "Thanks a lot for not ratting on me."

"Ah," Nancy said, her grin turning into a smile of truly evil glee. "That makes *three* you owe me now."

"Uh-oh," Frank said, shaking his head in sympathy. "Be afraid, Joe. Be *very* afraid."